The Courtesan's Maid

a Victorian romance saga

HOPE DAWSON

To girls and women everywhere
– past and present –
living in toil and hardship
yet never giving up hope
and always striving for a better tomorrow.

Chapter One

London, January 1864

Shivering with cold in her threadbare clothes, little Bess waited for the scrawny dog to finish doing its dirty business in the street. She knew she had to keep her distance or else the frightened mongrel would scurry off, depriving her of the smelly bounty she was after. The moment the dog was done defecating, Bess swooped in with her metal bucket.

But she wasn't alone. Old Charley appeared from the shadows as well, surprisingly fast for his age.

"I saw it first," the old man cackled as he viciously shoved her aside. Bess lost her balance and fell, sending her metal bucket rolling down the cobblestones with a loud clatter.

"No, you didn't," she yelled angrily while she got up on her feet again. "I spotted that dog two streets back and I followed it all this way."

But she was already too late as Charley scooped up the pure with his bare hands. At least she and

Nan used a small shovel, she thought, wrinkling her nose in disgust.

"But I got here sooner," he said triumphantly.

"Only because you pushed me," Bess replied. "You're a mean old man, Charley!"

"And you're nothing but a snot-faced little runt who should learn to show some respect to the elderly."

Bess briefly entertained the idea of giving *him* a rude shove and taking from his bucket what was rightfully hers. But she was only eight and despite old Charley's bony appearance, everyone knew he could kick harder than a mule.

"I'll tell Nan what you did," she snarled.

Charley grinned, revealing five brown teeth – the only ones he had left in his mouth. "Be sure to give old Meg my love, won't you?" He nodded a mocking goodbye at her and walked away, laughing to himself with that throaty cackle of his.

Bess kicked her empty bucket, sending it clattering further across the cobblestones. *Stupid Charley,* she grumbled silently. *Stupid pure.*

Being a pure finder was sad and humiliating enough already. She didn't need a mean old thief like him to make her job even worse. It would typically take her an entire day to fill her bucket with the faeces that the dogs of London left behind in the streets and alleys. And then the leather tanneries would only pay her a few pennies for her bucket of pure.

What a silly name for it, she thought with a wry smile. Whoever decided to call it that must have had a twisted sense of humour. Because the disgusting stuff was anything but pure. Especially when it had been sitting in a bucket all day long. It wasn't too bad in winter, but in the summer the heat and the buzzing flies made it almost unbearable.

At the moment however, her pure bucket was empty. And she didn't have the heart to start filling it. She hated this work. She hated this life. And she hated feeling cold and hungry all the time. She wanted to sit by a warm fire, with food in her belly and a roof over her head – the way it had been back when her parents and her brothers were still alive.

Now, her grandmother was all she had left. And they slept in a cold, damp corner of an abandoned factory by the river. It wasn't fair.

Bess clenched her fists into tight little balls of anger. She felt like kicking the bucket again, but she didn't want to risk damaging it. If she broke their bucket, Nan would be furious. So instead, she let her hands hang limply by her sides, dropped her shoulders and cried. *I'm so tired,* she wailed silently. Cold, tired and hungry.

"Stuff this pure," she decided. "I'll go to the market first." She didn't have any money to spend, but she enjoyed being in the busy crowd where she could watch people. There would be plenty of time to collect disgusting pure afterwards.

She didn't have to walk very far and she could hear the shouting voices of the costermongers before she saw their stalls. Strolling past the different vendors, a happy smile soon appeared on her face. She pictured herself as a well-dressed maid, out to buy food and groceries for her kind and wealthy mistress. In her hand she was no longer carrying a dirty old bucket, but a lovely wicker basket that would hold all her purchases. And instead of seeing her as a ragged little street rat, the stall holders were calling out to her, inviting her to try their goods and offering her their best prices.

Bess stopped by the stall of a baker. The smell of fresh bread and savoury pies was intoxicating. Closing her eyes, she breathed in deeply. The delicious scents entering her nose made her mouth water while her empty stomach was now growling even louder than before.

Opening her eyes again, she stared longingly at a pile of neatly stacked meat pies. They were small enough to hold in one hand and they looked so inviting. How she wished she could have one! And how unfortunate that she didn't have the money.

The baker didn't strike her as the type of man who would give her one for free, even if she begged and asked him nicely. But he seemed to be doing a brisk trade, so surely he could spare one tiny meat pie for a hungry young girl? She knew stealing was wrong, but her belly was screaming at her – pleading with her to eat something and silence the gnawing hunger.

So while the baker was distracted when he gave a woman her change, Bess' hand shot out and grabbed one of the smaller meat pies.

"Thief," the baker shouted.

Bess darted off as fast as she could, clutching the pie in her hand. And despite the baker's angry yells, nobody seemed to come chasing after her. She rounded a few corners and then ducked into a quiet alley. She had made it!

Her heart still pounding from her lucky escape, she leaned against a wall with her back to catch her breath. Then she held the stolen pie right underneath her nose, closed her eyes and took a good sniff of the delicious aroma.

"That pie looks tasty," a dark voice taunted. "Too bad you won't get to eat it."

Her eyes snapped open. Before her stood three grinning boys. She didn't know their names, but she had seen them around. They belonged to one of the gangs that ruled these streets. Instinctively, she lowered the pie in her hand and held it closer to her chest.

"It's mine," she said defiantly.

"Not really," the boy in the middle said. He looked a few years older than the other two, so he was probably in charge. "You stole that pie from the baker's. We heard him shouting and then we saw you running."

"What's it to you?"

"You shouldn't steal things."

"Ha! Since when do you care? I know who you are. Thieves and pickpockets!"

"That's right," the boy grinned menacingly. "And the market is ours. We don't take kindly to competition intruding on our territory. Do we, lads?" He threw a sideways glance at the younger boys to his left and right, who duly shook their heads and sniggered.

"I only grabbed this pie because I was hungry," Bess said defensively.

"It's still stealing," the boy replied. "And I'm afraid we can't let you do that. Joe?" He turned to the boy by his right shoulder and gestured towards Bess with a short nod of the head.

Joe stepped forward and held out his hand, with his palm facing up. "We'll take that, thank you very much." He was half a head taller than Bess and his hair was a fiery ginger.

"No," she said through gritted teeth. "It's mine. I'm not giving it to you."

"Don't be foolish, little girl. We'll–"

"Who are you calling a little girl, Freckle Face?"

"Freckle Face?! Why you dirty little–"

Joe made a move to grab her, but Bess bared her teeth and sunk them into his hand.

"Ouch! She bit me," he whimpered.

"Stop playing around and take that pie," the older boy ordered. "Or are you telling me you can't handle a little girl, Joe?" He laughed and the third boy joined in eagerly.

Joe's face hardened. Suddenly, he gave Bess a shove with his elbow while his other hand snatched the pie from her grip.

"You big, freckle-faced bully," she cried indignantly.

Joe handed the pie over to the older boy and then whipped around to Bess. "Call me Freckle Face one more time, little girl," he growled, "and I'll make you regret it. The name's Joe."

The leader of the trio took a bite from the meat pie and smiled. "Hmm, delicious." He broke off a piece and gave it to Joe. And then he gave another piece to the third boy. Pie crumbles and bits of meat fell on the ground, making Bess even more furious. They were deliberately wasting her pie! But she knew they had won and it would be useless to waste any more words or energy on them.

"Stick to collecting your pure, little girl," the leader smirked as he wiped his mouth. "And leave the stealing and thieving to the professionals."

Bess shot him an angry glare and she only stopped staring once they had disappeared from the alley. "Thieving cowards," she grumbled quietly. She couldn't go back to the market now, for risk of being recognised. But her belly was still empty. As empty as her bucket.

Chapter Two

When the clocks struck midday, Bess was still muttering to herself about the unfairness of it all. And she hadn't had much luck with finding pure either. Her bucket wasn't even a third of the way full. The cold was the worst thing of all though. A northerly wind drove temperatures below freezing point, while thick dark clouds made the day seem even more gloomy and depressing than it already was. Bess could feel the icy chill creeping into her bones. And every gust of bitter wind made her teeth chatter. But at least the freezing cold helped to distract her mind from the hunger in her stomach.

By two o'clock, she couldn't take much more. Her hands were blue and she had lost all sensation in her feet. She tried to warm herself by the open fires of several street vendors, but most shooed her away since she didn't look like she would be buying anything from them. And nobody wanted to be near the little girl with her smelly bucket anyway.

Exhausted and desperate, she dragged her numb feet and aching body to the one place where she knew she would be able to enjoy some warm shelter without bothering anyone – and without anyone bothering her.

The Grand Theatre wasn't nearly as grand as its name attempted to imply. The building had probably looked magnificent in the past, but those days were long gone. It was nice and warm inside however and that's exactly what had drawn Bess to it when she had first discovered the Grand several months earlier.

On a cold November afternoon, she had been looking for pure in the alley at the back of the theatre. And that's when the sound of laughter had caught her attention. A lively group of people – including the most beautiful woman Bess had ever seen – had walked past her and entered the theatre through the backdoor. They had seemed so cheerful and flamboyant to her, as if they were living in a much brighter world. Who were those people, she had wondered. And what made them so happy?

Curiosity had got the better of her and she'd decided she simply had to know the answer. Fed up with the cold, the idea of sneaking into the theatre had become irresistible. She had walked up to the backdoor and found it unlocked. With her heart beating wildly, she had slipped inside, careful to remain unseen by keeping to the shadows.

Hiding had turned out to be fairly easy in the old theatre. There were plenty of nooks and small dark spaces, not to mention a multitude of crates, props and furniture. It would have been a fun place for any adventurous eight-year-old. But for Bess, it had soon become her own little paradise: her secret sanctuary where she could escape, however briefly, from the unforgiving cold weather and from her cruel life on the street.

She found out that the happy people were actors, rehearsing a play they would be performing at the theatre. The beautiful woman was called Rebecca Sutcliffe, and most of the others in the group clearly adored her. Bess could see why. Not only was Miss Sutcliffe gorgeous and utterly charming, she turned out to be a talented actress as well. Bess loved to listen to the sound of Rebecca's voice and she dreamt of being able to attend a proper performance instead of having to lurk in the shadows.

Throughout the cold weeks and months that followed, Bess kept coming back to the theatre. She learned the actors' schedule and whenever they were at the theatre, she would sneak inside. Stealthy like an experienced burglar, but without ever stealing anything. Because that would have been wrong, she thought. Nobody knew she was there, and they wouldn't have hesitated to throw her out onto the street if they ever found out. But stealing from these people would have felt like betraying their hospitality. So all she ever did was hide in the darkness and enjoy the warm cosiness, while she listened to everything that went on in the theatre.

The best spot, but also the most dangerous one, was up in the rafters. They were like a crude wooden floor that extended over the entire stage, part of the wings and even some of the dressing rooms. Up there, Bess was able to hear every word that was said on stage, while she remained hidden from view. And through one of the many larger openings for the ropes and pulleys, she could even catch the occasional glimpse of the actors. She just had to mind her step and not move about too much.

Today, the actors were rehearsing a new play. Up in the rafters, Bess sat with her legs pulled up and her knees close to her chest, straining to hear the characters speaking their lines. The story seemed to be about a young orphaned woman from the slums, played by Miss Sutcliffe. There was also an evil landlord who was secretly in love with the woman.

Listening to their dialogues, Bess felt they didn't sound like any of the people from the slum she lived in. But then again, she supposed no one ever sounded like a real person in the theatre. She still loved every word of it though. Especially the part of Miss Sutcliffe. Her character seemed so vulnerable and yet so strong as she stood up to the wicked villain.

Maybe I should try to be more like her next time those street thugs decide to snatch something from me, she thought. In her mind, she imagined herself striking up a defiant pose and glaring bravely at the boy called Joe.

"This is ridiculous," an angry voice bristled on the stage below.

"What's the matter, Raymond darling?" Rebecca Sutcliffe asked.

"These lines of mine, they're rubbish," the man replied. "They make me sound like an imbecile. The audience will hate me with lines like that."

"But Raymond," another male voice said, "you're the villain. People are supposed to dislike your character."

Intrigued, Bess crawled towards the edge of one the holes in the floor so she could see what was going on below her.

"That's easy for you to say," the first man grumbled. "You get to play the love interest. They'll cheer you on for saving her, but boos and hisses is all I'll get."

"You're being silly, Raymond," Rebecca Sutcliffe said with a radiant smile. "Theatre is all about strong emotions. It's what the people want."

"Bah, humbug!"

Rebecca giggled. "Now you sound like a naughty schoolboy who's angry for not getting his way. If I didn't know any better, I'd be inclined to think you were jealous."

"Jealous?! Me? Ha, there's a laugh. Why would I be jealous of you? I might be twice your age, young lady, but I'm at least three times as talented."

Even from her position high up, Bess could see the smile vanish from Miss Sutcliffe's face.

"There's no need to be mean, Raymond," Rebecca said icily.

"She's right, Raymond," a third man spoke up. Bess recognised the voice of the producer, Walter Huxley. "I think you owe Rebecca an apology for a flippant remark like that."

"So it's three against one, eh? Well, in that case, see how you get on without me. Adieu!" Turning up his nose, the actor walked off the stage.

"Raymond," Rebecca called after him. "Don't be such a buffoon and come back."

Bess heard a door slam. This was almost as entertaining as watching the actual play, she thought guiltily. She leaned in even closer, so she could see how Miss Sutcliffe was taking it.

"Walter, what will we do now?" the actress asked, letting out an exasperated sigh as she sat down.

"Don't you worry, my dear," he said while stepping onto the stage. "We'll find another actor to replace Raymond. Someone who's more appreciative of your enormous talent."

He took Rebecca's hand and patted it tenderly. From her viewpoint above, Bess noticed the top of his head was growing bald.

"If you say so, Walter," Rebecca answered. He stood beside her and as she glanced up, her eyes suddenly focused on the little girl peering down at them from the rafters.

Startled, Bess gave a silent gasp and quickly retreated into the safety of the shadows again. But in doing so, she made the old floorboards creak.

"Wh– What was that?" she heard Walter ask nervously. "Did you hear that noise?"

"Probably just rats, darling," Rebecca said.

Bess sighed with relief, but she decided it was better for her to sneak out of the theatre before anyone came up to take a closer look. Without making a single sound, she slipped outside and retrieved her pure bucket from where she had hidden it.

"Not even half full," she grumbled. "Nan will be so cross with me."

Dusk came early on these short winter days and Bess realised she didn't have time to go searching for more pure. She needed to take what little she had in her bucket and head to the leather tanneries before they closed. She would worry about her grandmother's reaction later.

Walking through the cold and rapidly darkening streets, one thought intrigued her. Miss Sutcliffe had seen her spying on them. Their eyes had met, briefly – she was sure of that. And yet, the actress hadn't betrayed her. Bess didn't know why. But she loved the fact that the two of them were now sharing a little secret.

Chapter Three

"You lazy good-for-nothing! Is that all you've made today? Even with my bad legs I could have earned three times as much."

Wrapped up in grimy blankets and lying on an improvised straw mattress on the bare floor, Nan looked at the coins in the open palm of her hand and then glanced up at Bess. Her old eyes didn't see half as well as they used to, but right now they seemed like deep pools filled with hateful contempt. And they were firmly fixed on her granddaughter.

"I'm sorry, Nan," Bess said, lowering her gaze so she didn't have to look into those dark eyes.

"Sorry isn't good enough. Sorry won't put food in our empty bellies, will it?"

Bess shook her head meekly. She felt like a fool for having neglected her duties. She had known that Nan would be angry at her if she didn't sell at least one full bucket of pure. But still she had chosen to sneak into the theatre for a while. Which, she supposed, made her twice a fool.

"How come you only made so little?" her grandmother demanded.

I could try to make up a story about someone stealing my pure, she thought. *Maybe I could blame it on old Charley.* But she quickly decided against that avenue. The situation was bad enough as it was. Telling lies would only make matters worse.

"I– I got distracted," she said.

"Distracted, eh? I take it that means you were loafing about and daydreaming again. You'd rather play than work hard, wouldn't you? But nobody's going to pay you for that, are they?"

Unless you happen to work in the theatre, Bess thought. Even in her mind she couldn't help escaping to that safe and happy dream world.

"I don't know what I've done to deserve such a lazy grandchild," Nan snarled. "You're too much like your mother, that's the problem. I warned my poor John –God rest his soul– I warned him not to marry that woman. But would he listen to me? No, of course he wouldn't!"

Bess had heard this rant before. Nan had never approved of Mother, and she often went so far as to blame her daughter-in-law for the horrible disease that had killed Bess' family. Even though Father had been the first to fall ill and die.

"I'll do better tomorrow, Nan. I promise."

"You can't do much worse than this, that's for sure." Her grandmother held up the coins as if they were a personal insult to her. "We can't buy supper with this. And how am I supposed to drive the chill from these old bones of mine without my medicine?"

Bess held her tongue. Ale and brandy hardly counted as medicine. But she didn't want to make Nan even angrier, so she kept that thought to herself.

"Run off to the square and get us something for free from the soup kitchen if they're still there," Nan grumbled. "And drop by the pub on your way back. See what they'll give you for this pittance," she said, handing back the money.

"And don't you dare moan about being hungry," she added with a sneer. "It'll be a good lesson to you. Maybe with a rumbling stomach you'll try harder to earn a living for us. If it weren't for my legs and my back, I'd show you what hard work looked like."

"I need to hurry before the soup kitchen runs out of food," Bess said quickly. That was true, but it was also a convenient excuse to escape Nan's stern sermon.

Cautiously picking her way past the small groups of homeless people with whom they shared the rundown factory building, she avoided making eye contact with anyone. Some of their fellow slum dwellers tended to be unpredictable or downright mad. But as Bess had learned, if she kept herself to herself and didn't engage with them, they usually left her in peace.

Half an hour later, she returned with cold watery soup for the two of them and a half pint of ale for Nan. They ate in silence, with Bess feeling grateful for the ale, since it helped to make her grandmother less grumpy. After having finished their meagre supper, they settled down for the night.

"Good night, Nan," she said softly.

But a grumbling slur was the only reply she got.

Despite rolling up into a ball and wrapping her blanket around her tightly, Bess still shivered. She wished they could have had a small fire to keep the freezing viciousness of the night at bay. They never had enough money to buy coal however, and any firewood they could have salvaged from the building had long ago been stripped away by others. Sleep didn't come easy under these circumstances, but eventually exhaustion got the better of her.

In the morning, she woke up with a headache and a gnawing hunger in her belly. She rose quickly, moving and stretching in an attempt to get some warmth flowing through her body. Nan was snoring lightly and Bess didn't bother to wake her up. Fearing her grandmother would be in a foul mood, she also knew Nan probably wouldn't be joining her anyway due to her weak legs and failing health.

So after she had folded and tucked away her blanket, she ventured outside on her own – determined to make more money than the day before.

By noon, she had already managed to fill her first bucket of pure. The money she got for it from the tannery felt like a small fortune to her.

But that flicker of hope was promptly dashed to pieces. Because when she went to the market for a fresh loaf of bread that she could share with Nan, it cost her nearly all the money she had.

This won't do, she complained bitterly to herself. Every penny she and Nan earned, they were immediately forced to spend on food. And that was just to keep them from starving. How did others do it, she wondered? How did they have money left over to spend on clothes and nice things?

Clutching her loaf of bread in her hands, she stopped and watched the people strolling around at the market. Most of them seemed a lot happier too, she thought.

Take that fancy gentleman with the top hat, she said. *I bet he's never had to collect pure. And yet, his pockets are probably bulging with money. No wonder he's got such a big smile on his face.*

His kind breezed through life without a care in the world. While for poor folk like herself, every day was a struggle for survival. What made them so special? Didn't she deserve a bit more happiness too?

She didn't want much. They could keep their big houses and expensive togs. She would be perfectly content with nothing but a few more coins jingling in her pocket. Just so she and Nan wouldn't need to worry about how they were going to afford food. Maybe for a week or so. How wonderful that would be!

She watched as the gentleman took out a leather pouch to pay for a fruit scone from one of the market stalls.

See, she sighed. *For him, it's loose change in his pocket. But I'm sure Nan and I could eat and stay warm for days with that sort of money.*

A hard look came over her face as an idea began to take shape in her mind. It was a bad and wicked idea, she realised all too well. But if she had to choose between that and another night of freezing and starving, then stealing a handful of coins from a rich man seemed like the lesser of two evils to her.

Chapter Four

Cautiously, Bess started following the gentleman at a distance while she tried to think of the best way to get her hands on the money in his pouch. How did the pickpockets do it? They made it look so easy and the victim hardly ever noticed what was happening until it was too late.

That's where she had gone wrong yesterday, she decided. She had simply grabbed that pie and run off, causing the baker to yell and scream after her.

She needed to be sneakier this time. Even more so if she didn't want to attract the attention of any gang members. But how? She couldn't just walk up to the man and slide her hand into his pocket. Only an experienced pickpocket was able to pull off that sort of trick.

Her thoughts were rudely interrupted when someone knocked into her and she dropped her loaf of bread.

"You clumsy oaf," she said to the boy who was smaller and younger than her. "Look what you've done."

Suddenly, another boy snatched up her loaf and took off with it. "Oi," she shouted.

"Should've paid better attention," the first boy said with a mocking smirk on his grubby face. "The market's a dangerous place, you know." In a taunting salute to her, he touched the rim of his flat cap that was too big for his head and then he hurried off after his thieving friend.

This hadn't been an accident! Those sly little thugs had bumped into her on purpose, with the intent of stealing her bread. She had worked all morning... and now she didn't have anything to show for it. As she stood there empty-handed, she felt tears welling up in her eyes.

No, she growled, stomping an angry foot on the cobblestones. *Crying won't give me my bread back.*

Having chased her tears away, she wiped her nose on her sleeve and looked around for the fancy gentleman. Any qualms she might have had about picking his pocket were firmly gone.

And now she had a good idea how to do it. Thanks to those two boys, she thought with an impish grin. Since she didn't stand a chance of stealing the man's money unnoticed, she would bump into him. He'd be too startled to feel her hand taking the pouch out of his pocket. Or so she hoped.

Bess spotted her mark and began trailing him again. In her head she pictured the scene, rehearsing the entire routine from start to finish several times. Being quick and acting innocent were the most important things, she thought.

She was just a silly young girl – too foolish and too distracted to mind where she was going. *Oh, pardon me, sir,* she would say. *I'm so terribly sorry, sir.*

He would grumble and tell her off, but she would already have grabbed his pouch and hid it in the folds of her dress before he even turned round to face her. She would lower her head respectfully, mumble another apology and then walk away – calmly, as if nothing else had happened.

It was a simple plan, but the best plans always were.

Taking a deep breath, she wiped her sweaty hands dry on her skirt. *Stop dilly-dallying and get it over with, Bess,* she egged herself on. When she swallowed, she could feel her heart thumping nervously in her throat.

The gentleman was now only a few paces ahead of her and she kept her eyes firmly fixed on his back. When he stopped to look at a stall selling colourful boiled sweets in large glass jars, Bess seized her chance. With a quick dash, she closed the short distance between them and bumped into him. Her hand immediately slipped into his pocket and found his pouch. She briskly extracted the money, but then she fumbled with the folds of her dress. This forced her to hold the pouch in her hands and hide them behind her back, just as the angry gentleman rounded on her.

"You blundering fool," he bristled. "Mind where you're going, you smelly guttersnipe!"

"I'm terribly sorry, sir," she stuttered, her face red with shame and trepidation. The pouch felt heavy and very big in her trembling hands.

"I could have tripped and hurt myself because of you. Or I could have knocked over some of these glass jars. A fine mess that would have made."

"Forgive me, sir," she said, taking a small step backwards. They were already attracting too much attention to her liking. She needed to beat a quiet retreat before anyone noticed the leather pouch she was holding behind her back.

A few more words, she thought. *A few more steps. Then I can turn around and leave.*

"I promise to be more careful in future, sir," she muttered while she lowered her eyes and slowly backed away.

Almost there...

Keeping the pouch out of the man's sight, she turned round and promptly bumped into a dark uniform with a single row of shiny silver buttons.

"You're nicked, sweetheart," the constable said as he placed a heavy hand on her tiny shoulder.

Her heart started racing and she broke out in a cold sweat, but she tightened her nervous grip on the pouch.

"I didn't do anything wrong," she lied.

"So that gentleman's purse just happened to find its way from his pocket into your hands by accident, did it?" the constable sneered.

"Purse?" the man asked with obvious surprise. His hand moved to his pocket and found it empty. "Good heavens! That miserable urchin took my money."

"She had been following you like a shadow, sir. But I can spot her kind from a mile away. Developed quite the nose for it, I have." He tapped the side of his sizeable nose with his finger. "So when she struck, I stood ready."

"I'm most indebted to you, sir," the man said, looking down on Bess with self-righteous disdain.

"That's what the police are for, sir. Now then–" The constable turned to Bess. "You will give this nice gentleman's purse back and then you and I are going to take a lovely stroll down to the police station."

"Never," she growled with the intensity of a wild animal that found itself trapped. She had got so close to her prize, she wasn't prepared to give it up without a fight.

"Now look here," the constable said. But before he could finish his sentence, Bess kicked him hard in the shin. Crying out in pain, he swore profusely.

He also loosened his grip on her shoulder however, which was all Bess needed to make her escape. Holding the pouch in her clenched fists, she darted off – with a furious constable hot on her heels.

"Stop," he shouted. "Thief! In the name of the Law! Someone stop that child."

But most onlookers merely stared and gawked in surprise or half-hidden glee, as people were wont to do. And even if anyone had tried to intervene, Bess was moving much too swiftly for them.

She knew though that she wouldn't be able to keep up this breakneck speed indefinitely. Her sides were beginning to hurt and it would only be a matter of time until the policeman caught up with her. But she didn't dare look over her shoulder, so instead she continued to flee blindly through the maze of winding and narrow streets.

Suddenly, two hands grabbed her from behind and pushed her into an alleyway. "Keep running," a boy's voice breathed hotly in her ear while the hands didn't let go of her.

Before the policeman had rounded the corner of the alley, Bess was shoved through an open cellar door. Someone jumped down next to her and hurriedly let the doors fall shut behind them. Before the daylight vanished, she recognised her saviour.

"Joe–" she started.

His hands flew to her mouth to silence her. "Quiet," he whispered.

Breathing rapidly, she listened to the heavy footsteps of the constable on the cobblestones outside. He ran past the closed cellar door for several yards and then stopped. Realising he had lost her, he swore and muttered as he kicked at some rubbish that littered the alley.

"Did you see a young girl running through here?" he asked a few people. But in this part of town, no one was much inclined to be of service to the loathed constabulary. Keeping very still in their hiding place, Bess and Joe heard the policeman swear a bit more until his voice began to trail off. Only when Joe was satisfied the peeler had left, did he remove his hand from her mouth. Bess took a deep breath and then let out a long sigh of relief.

"What is it you stole this time?" he asked. In the gloomy cellar she couldn't make out his face. But she heard the mockery in his voice.

"None of your business."

"As we explained to you only yesterday, stealing is very much our business."

"I'll bite your hand off if you try to take it from me."

He sniggered. "I believe you would."

"And is that why you saved me?" she sneered. "Just so you could have my prize for yourself? I'd rather have been caught by that policeman than hand over the money to you."

"So it's money you took?"

She cursed herself for letting that piece of information slip. He merely laughed.

"You're making good progress. Yesterday it was just a pie, today it's money. Will you be robbing a jewellery shop next?"

"What do you want, Joe?"

"I want a share of the loot."

"Forget it."

He sighed. "Listen, if you want to be a thief on these streets, you have to give a share to the folks in charge. Those are the rules of our gang."

"You're not in charge and I don't want to be in your gang. I just needed some money to buy food for me and my Nan."

"Only members of the gang are allowed to steal. We don't like having any competition. Show me what you've got."

He opened one of the cellar doors to let more light in. She blinked and clutched the pouch to her chest.

"That looks like a juicy purse," he nodded approvingly. "Well done."

"The owner didn't feel a thing when I snatched it," she said with defiant pride. "I would have got away with it too, if that policeman hadn't spotted me."

"I can see you have a talent for the trade. You really should join our gang. I'd be happy to put in a good word for you."

She shook her head. "I'm not a thief."

"Yet," he added and laughed. "But enough fooling about. I still want my share."

Bess eyed him suspiciously. "How much do you want?"

"Since this is your first time, I'll be nice. That leather purse itself will fetch a good price, if you know who to sell it to. You keep the coins and I'll take the purse. Do we have a deal?"

She hesitated, wondering if perhaps he was playing games with her. But a rumbling noise in her tummy reminded her of the urgency of her situation.

"All right," she said.

"Smart girl," he smiled. "Let's have it then."

He held out his hand, but she didn't trust him and so she carefully shook the coins into her hand and tossed him the empty pouch.

"Thanks," he said, admiring it. "What's your name?"

"Bess."

"Pleasure doing business with you, Bess. Whenever you want to join our gang, just come and find me."

"No, thank you."

He shrugged. "It's a better life than collecting pure. Until next time, Bess." He winked, climbed up the stairs and disappeared into the alley.

There won't be a next time, she thought, not entirely sure of her own words. But the coins in her hand felt good.

That evening, she and Nan filled their bellies with more food and drink than they usually had in an entire week. And even then Bess still had plenty of coins left over.

If Nan had any doubts about how her granddaughter had obtained so much money, she didn't mention them. Instead, she eagerly accepted the brandy Bess had bought for her.

"Just what my aching old body needed," she sighed happily after another swig from her bottle. "I feel ten years younger. Why, I might even get up tomorrow and come with you. Not that you seem to need my help," she chuckled. "You did really well today, dear."

Bess said nothing and gnawed on the chicken bone she was holding.

Yes, she had done well, she thought. But the warm glow in her belly couldn't quite drown out the pang of guilt she was feeling.

Chapter Five

The next morning, Bess woke up with a smile. Because even though her thin blanket hadn't done much to protect her from the freezing cold, at least she wasn't hungry for a change. And she'd had the most beautiful dream: dressed in fancy new clothes, she had visited the theatre on the opening night of Rebecca Sutcliffe's latest play. Sitting radiantly in her own opera box, men and women admired her magnificent outfit and nodded at her, eager to catch her eye. Reminiscing about her dream, she let out a long and happy sigh.

But the sight of her own breath turning into a small cloud of icy mist in the cold morning air quickly brought her mind back to reality. With a reluctant groan, she got up from underneath her blanket and began to fold it.

"Morning, Nan," she called out to her grandmother. "Time to get up now."

When there was no response from the curled up figure lying close to her, Bess spoke up a little louder. "Morning, Nan!"

Her hearing sure is getting worse, she thought when her grandmother didn't stir. "Are you feeling up to joining me today?" Bess virtually shouted. "Or would you rather stay here?"

Still no answer.

"Nan?"

Bess knelt down and placed a hand on her grandmother's shoulder to give it a gentle nudge. But the old woman felt cold and stiff to the touch. *Lifeless,* an alarming thought told her.

She shook more firmly and then pulled back the blanket. Bess let out a frightened shriek when she saw Nan's face: it was very pale –almost white– and with a hint of blue.

"Nan!"

Bess grabbed hold of her grandmother, but deep down she knew nothing would wake her up anymore. Nan was gone for good.

Frozen to death during the night, her mind stated blankly. Then the reality of what had happened sank in and her tears began to flow.

"Nana Morgan, what will I do without you?" she sobbed, sitting on her knees beside her grandmother's dead body.

Nan hadn't always been the easiest person to live with, and they had often argued over many things. But Nan was the only family Bess had left.

And the only grown-up to look after her in this world. Now however, Bess was all alone.

How was a little girl like her supposed to survive on her own? What could she do?

I'll just have to carry on, I guess, she thought as she glanced over her shoulder at the shadows surrounding her, painfully aware of how helpless she was. She felt like a frightened animal, nervous that at any moment some vicious predator might appear out of nowhere.

Without her Nan, how would she stand a chance against the other tramps and homeless people? As soon as they realised Old Meg wasn't around anymore, wouldn't the thugs try to take advantage of her situation? They could rob her of everything she had and she wouldn't be able to defend herself.

Maybe Joe was right. Maybe she was better off joining their gang. He did say she seemed to have a talent for picking pockets. But did she really want to be a thief for the rest of her life? Stealing that gentleman's money had been an act of desperation – something she had done out of anger, frustration and hunger. She knew stealing and thieving were wrong, and she didn't plan on making it a regular habit.

And besides, with only herself to look after, the pennies she earned in an honest way would go a lot further.

Immediately horrified by her own train of thought, she gasped and covered her mouth. *What a terrible thing to think,* she admonished herself. How could she sit here by the dead body of her poor grandmother and take comfort from the fact there was a mouth less to feed? Surely, only a monster would think such things?

"Bad bad bad Bess," she hissed under her breath. "What a wicked child you are."

This was all her fault. She had stolen somebody's money and God had punished her for her crime by taking Nan away from her. She was to blame for Nan's death, she told herself. And now she had to find a way to make it right. Nothing could bring Nana back to her of course. But maybe if she let God know that she was very sorry, then He wouldn't punish her any further?

"What do you do when you've made God angry and you want to apologise?" she asked herself. She snapped her fingers when the answer came to her. "Church! You go to church."

There was one close by, she knew. She should go there straight away and pray. She had stopped going to church after her parents died and she didn't remember any of the prayers. But she still knew what to do: you knelt down and folded your hands. If she said a few words, that would probably do the trick, wouldn't it? Or would God be expecting a proper prayer from her, even if she was only eight? She decided she'd find out when she got there.

"I have to go now, Nan," Bess said to the frozen body on the ground. "I'm sorry for being naughty and I promise to do better from now on. No more stealing."

She wiped her nose, got up and looked at her dead grandmother one last time, before leaving their hiding place in the crumbling factory building and heading for the local church.

Someone will have to bury Nan, she thought as she passed through the tall porch and entered the church. Perhaps she could ask the priest to take care of that.

Inside, everything was quiet and peaceful. A few candles were burning, but to her relief Bess seemed to be the only one there. She felt ill at ease in this place of worship, convinced that street rats like her didn't belong here.

The quicker I get this over with, the better, she told herself while she hurried over to the large crucifix that stood on a pedestal at the back of the church.

She knelt down by its feet, folded her hands and cleared her throat.

But how was she supposed to address the man on the cross? She couldn't remember what he was called and she wasn't sure if you were even allowed to use his name to his face.

I haven't started yet and I'm already making a mess of it, she whimpered tearfully. *There's no chance God will forgive me this way.*

Frowning and angry with herself, she glanced up at the figure on the cross, half expecting Him to be looking down on her with an annoyed glare. Luckily, the man simply seemed to be waiting for her to speak.

"Hello, Sir," she began, trying to sound as respectful as she could. "I've come to say I'm sorry. I shouldn't have picked that gentleman's pocket yesterday. I knew it was wrong, but I was so hungry and my Nan was ill and he looked like he had plenty of money, so I thought it wouldn't hurt him too much if I took the coins he had on him."

She paused, but the man on the cross remained silent.

"And now my Nana is dead. Because of what I did. I suppose I deserved to be punished, but I didn't think You'd take my Nan. Please look after her in heaven. She can be a bit grumpy sometimes, but in her heart she's good."

The man on the cross didn't reply, but Bess thought he looked more friendly.

"Anyway, that's why I came here this morning. To say I'm terribly sorry and that I promise I'll never steal anything ever again in my life."

She took all the money out of her pocket and carefully laid the coins on the pedestal of the crucifix.

"This is what's left of the money I stole. I'll leave it here with You. I know You have no use for money of course, but maybe You can give it to someone who needs it more than I do."

"What a wonderful idea," a voice said.

Bess jumped up and spun round, her eyes wide with terror and her heart beating wildly.

"I'm sorry," the young priest smiled. "I didn't mean to startle you. But that was a lovely prayer you just said, my dear."

Bess felt her cheeks blush with shame. "You heard everything?"

"Not all of it and I didn't mean to listen in," the priest answered kindly. "But I saw you sitting here as I walked in and I didn't want to disturb you, so I kept very quiet."

"Oh," she said awkwardly.

"Don't worry," he chuckled, seeing her discomfort. "I won't tell anyone how you obtained the money. That will remain a secret between you and our Good Lord. And you've already done the right thing, so I'm sure He will forgive you for your trespass."

"Do you think so?"

"Of course He will. But tell me, child. Did you say your grandmother passed away?"

Bess nodded. "She died last night. We live in the abandoned factory by the river, you see. And it got really cold in the night."

"May her soul rest in peace," he said, shaking his sorrowful head. "Have you got any other family?"

"None, sir. My parents and my brothers died when I was little. So it was just me and Nan."

"You poor thing." He tilted his head to the side as he regarded her with pity in his eyes.

"And I haven't even got any money to bury her," she said, fighting back a fresh wave of tears.

"The parish can see to that. So don't you worry, my sweet child. But first, we must find you a new home. Come," he said, holding out his hand to her. "I know just the place."

An instant sense of alarm pushed away any grief or sadness she was feeling. "I don't want a new home."

"But you have nowhere to live. And you're much too young to survive on your own. You'll have lots of other children to play with at the workhouse."

"The workhouse?" Bess was horrified. She had heard the stories. The place was like a prison where they made you work hard, no matter how old you were. And all they ever fed you was sloppy gruel, thin soup and mouldy crusts of stale bread. She was convinced she would be better off living on the street.

"It's the best place for a lonely orphan like yourself," the priest said, stepping in closer. But before he could take her hand, Bess ran past him as fast as she could and fled outside. The priest called after her, but she didn't stop running until she was several streets away from the church.

The workhouse was no good, she decided. There was only one place in the world where she felt happy and safe. And that was in the theatre, hiding in some dark corner while Miss Sutcliffe stood on stage, rehearsing one of her roles.

Before she knew it, her feet were taking her in the direction of the alley behind the Grand. The theatre would probably still be deserted this early in the day, she realised. But she knew how to gain access. If you were brave and determined enough, there was always a way in. Climbing up the drainpipe was her favourite route. It was dangerous, but she didn't care if she fell to her death.

No one would care.

She found an unlocked window on one of the upper floors and let herself in. As she had guessed, there wasn't anyone around – which suited her perfectly. After the unnerving events that morning, she welcomed a bit of peace and quiet. Much like a dear friend wrapping a soothing arm around her, the darkness completely enveloped her, inviting her to make herself comfortable.

I'll sit here for a while and think about what to do next. Yes, that sounded like a good idea to her. Have a little rest first. Maybe even shut her eyes for a bit. Not too long though. She couldn't let anyone catch her here.

But the moment Bess closed her eyelids, she drifted off into a deep and troubled sleep.

Chapter Six

A hard kick to the leg jolted her wide awake with a frightening start. "Who are you?" an angry-faced man towering over her demanded. "And what are you doing here?"

Bess recognised him as Walter Huxley, the theatre producer she had seen and heard many times during her secret break-ins. To her own horror, she realised she must have fallen asleep where she had sat down.

And now she had been found out.

Before she had time to say anything or to think of an excuse, Mr Huxley grabbed her by the ear and pulled her to her feet. Terrorised, Bess howled in agony at the searing pain.

"You're hurting me," she screamed through hot tears. "Let go!" She was vaguely aware of other people rushing to the source of all this commotion.

"Walter, what's going on?" a sweet voice full of concern asked. Bess saw it was Rebecca Sutcliffe, surrounded by some of the other theatre people.

Now her shame and humiliation were complete, she thought.

"I caught this disgusting street rat taking a nap here," the producer said with clear disdain, still holding Bess by the ear. "No, I take that back. At least rats can serve a useful purpose in the dog baiting dens. This... thing is even less than a rat."

He scowled at her and twisted her ear, making her scream out in pain again.

"Walter," the actress spoke sternly. "You're hurting the poor little girl."

"The poor little girl was probably planning to rob us all, Rebecca." He brought his face closer to Bess and growled, "Weren't you, you little weasel?"

"Walter!" Miss Sutcliffe stamped her foot.

The producer let go of his prey and as Bess' hands flew up to cover her throbbing ear, Miss Sutcliffe immediately stepped over to take Bess in her arms.

"Look, the poor darling is shivering with fright," she said, admonishing her producer.

"She's just feigning," he shrugged.

"As an actress, I can usually tell when someone is feigning, you know. And this poor little angel seems genuinely petrified." She turned to Bess and gently lifted up the girl's face between her tender hands. "Aren't you, my little darling?"

Bess nodded, slightly afraid and unsure what to make of this. But as soon as she glanced up at Miss Sutcliffe's mesmerising green eyes, she felt herself relax a little bit.

"Say," the actress smiled. "You look familiar. Have we met before?"

She knows, Bess thought as panic took hold of her once more. *She knows it was me she saw spying on her from the rafters.*

She felt ashamed and wanted to stare at the floor. But those green eyes drew her gaze. She expected to see dislike or disapproval in them. Instead, all she saw was kindness.

"Yes, you've seen me before, Miss Sutcliffe," she answered timidly.

"You know my name?" The smile on Miss Sutcliffe's face grew even broader and brighter.

"Ha," Mr Huxley scoffed. "Everyone knows your name, Rebecca."

Casting a quick sideways glare at her producer, Miss Sutcliffe turned back to Bess with those captivating eyes of hers. "How did we meet, little one?"

"We didn't really meet, Miss Sutcliffe." Convinced those green eyes would see right through any lies, Bess decided honesty was her best option at this point. "But I've been coming here since a while and I've watched you on stage many times."

"A fan," the actress purred. "How delightful."

"Preposterous," Mr Huxley snorted. "Look at how she's dressed. People like her don't visit the theatre. They can't afford the ticket. And even if they could, they'd sooner spend their money on drinking and gambling."

"Stop being such a rude boor, Walter. We shouldn't judge people by their appearance."

Bess swallowed. "I, um– I don't really visit when there's a performance in the evening, Miss. I've been sneaking in here, because it's so cosy and warm." Blushing, she pointed at the rafters above their heads. "It was me up there earlier this week."

"I knew it," Mr Huxley hissed. "I knew it wasn't a rat! How long have you been doing this, you nasty little weasel?"

"Walter–"

"A couple of months," Bess confessed.

"Good Lord," he gasped. "And all this time you have been spying on us from the shadows? That's horrendous! The mere thought of it sends cold shivers up my spine."

"What spine?" someone muttered behind his back.

"I wasn't spying," Bess replied with fierce intensity. "Honest. I was just curious and it was very cold outside. But then I heard Miss Sutcliffe for the first time during one of your rehearsals. And I really liked her. So I came back many more times after that. Mostly for her."

She blushed and turned to her idol. "It's true, Miss. I just love to listen and watch when you play."

"Oh, you precious little darling!"

"Lies," Mr Huxley sneered. "Filthy, rotten lies. She probably pilfered anything she could lay her grubby hands on."

"I never did! I swear."

"And just think of the dangers and diseases she has exposed us to. She could have given us lice. Or worse."

"Calm your nerves, Walter. I know you're a theatre producer, but that doesn't mean you should turn everything into a drama, darling."

He opened his mouth to reply, but the chuckling laughter of the rest of the troupe quickly silenced him.

"Tell me, little one," Miss Sutcliffe asked. "Where do you live?"

"Nowhere in particular," Bess replied, feeling ashamed. "Lately, my Nan and I have been sleeping in an old abandoned factory."

Mr Huxley made a condescending tutting noise, but one look from Rebecca made him hold his tongue.

"So you have no real home?"

Bess shook her head. "No, Miss. Just a sleeping spot in that factory building. And now I don't even know if I want to go back there."

"Why is that, dear?"

"Because–" She took a deep breath and said, "Because last night, Nan died in her sleep."

"How awful! That must have upset you and your family a great deal."

"I don't have any family," Bess said as her voice cracked. "They all died a few years ago. Nan was all I had left."

"You poor darling," Miss Sutcliffe gasped, pulling Bess close to her. "I know what it's like to lose your parents. My papa and mama died in an accident when I was sixteen."

Bess looked up with big eyes full of surprise. "Did you end up on the street as well, Miss?"

"No, dear. My sister and I were lucky. Our grandmother took us in and looked after us." She smiled at Bess and added, "So it would seem you and I have something in common."

Bess' mouth dropped open in surprise. Miss Sutcliffe was an orphan too!

Mr Huxley cleared his throat. "Look here. This is all very touching, but we have a rehearsal to be getting on with. If the little urchin has no one to turn to, I'm sure the orphanage or the workhouse will take her."

"No," Bess blurted out as her body stiffened and her eyes instinctively searched for the quickest escape route. "That's where the priest wanted to take me as well. But I'm not going! The workhouse is a horrible place."

"Nonsense," Mr Huxley said. "They'll give you clean clothes, a bed to sleep in and three meals a day. For free no less. What more could a homeless little tramp like you ask for?"

"That's not what I heard," Bess shot back. "And I'm not a tramp! The workhouse is a prison where everyone is mean to you. I'd rather be free and live on the street than be forced to do what someone else tells me to do all the time, just to have a place to sleep and a bowl of gruel."

"Beggars can't be choosers," he sniffed haughtily.

"I'm not going to the workhouse," Bess said decisively. She readied herself to make a dash for the door, but Rebecca stopped her.

"Perhaps there's no need for that, my little one," the actress smiled in that enchantingly charming way of hers. Bess hesitated, unable to move while those green eyes peered down into her heart.

"What's your name, dear?"

"Bess, Miss. Bess Morgan."

"You seem like a clever girl to me, Bess. You must be, if you've survived on the street for so long."

"I can hold my own, I guess," she shrugged. "The gangs are the most trouble."

"I'm sure they are. Well, Bess, it just so happens that I have been thinking about hiring an assistant. Someone to run errands for me and do a spot of cooking, cleaning and mending."

"Rebecca," Mr Huxley gasped in shock. "You're not seriously thinking of hiring this little street rat, are you?"

"Oh, do be quiet, Walter. Do you think you could do that for me, Bess?"

"I–" Lost for words, she opened and closed her mouth. But Miss Sutcliffe's friendly face was impossible to say no to. "I don't know, Miss. I can cook a little bit, and cleaning probably isn't too hard. But I can't sew or mend, I'm afraid."

"You'll learn quickly enough. Do you want the position? I can't pay you much, but you would have room and board." She leaned in closer and winked. "That means a bed to sleep in and food to eat."

Bess felt her jaw drop. She couldn't believe what she was hearing.

"Rebecca, are you mad?!" Mr Huxley fumed. "She'll rob you blind. Worse yet, she might kill you in your sleep."

"I'm growing tired of your hysterics, Walter. And if you don't cease this nonsense of yours, I swear I shan't speak to you for a week."

Leaving him to sulk like a schoolboy who's been told off for being naughty, she flashed Bess an amused grin. "So what do you say, dear?"

"You want... me," Bess stuttered incredulously, "to come live with you?"

Rebecca nodded. "I would need to have my assistant with me at all times, obviously."

"Oh, thank you, Miss Sutcliffe," she exclaimed as she threw her arms around the actress's waist. "I promise to work hard and I'll learn to do everything you need from me."

Several members of the troupe gave a little cheer, while Walter Huxley threw dark and jealous glares at Bess.

"That's settled then," Rebecca said. "And now, my good people, we have a play to prepare for."

The rest of the afternoon, Bess watched the actors rehearse – not from the shadows up in the rafters, but from a comfortable front row seat.

Maybe the priest was right, she thought, not once taking her eyes off Miss Sutcliffe. Perhaps the man on the cross had indeed forgiven her.

If this is a dream, I hope I never wake up.

She pinched herself a couple of times to make sure. But the pain was real, which for once in her life made her smile.

Chapter Seven

Riding a hired hansom cab late at night, Bess sat squeezed in between Miss Sutcliffe and Mr Huxley. Her eyelids were growing heavy and she was struggling to stay awake. She had never ridden in a horse-driven carriage before, so this trip should have excited her. But the day had been a long and eventful one. And on top of that, they had all gone out for a big meal after the rehearsal.

So despite the rattling and shaking of the cab, Bess was finding it hard to stop herself from falling asleep. Her head kept dropping slowly to the side, where it landed against the soft shoulder of Miss Sutcliffe.

"Thank you for offering to share your cab with us, Walter darling," the actress said. As Bess closed her tired eyes, Rebecca's voice sounded like a lullaby to her ears.

"My pleasure, dear," he said. "No need for you to bear the expense when your room is only a small detour on my way home." He was trying to be friendly to Rebecca, but he looked uncomfortable while covering his mouth and nose with his handkerchief.

"Is anything the matter?" the actress asked. "You're not feeling unwell, are you?"

"It's this street rat of yours," he complained. "She smells as if she lives in the sewers."

"She's not a rat, Walter."

"Well, she smells like one."

"That's nothing a bath won't fix. Stop being so squeamish. It's rather off-putting, you know."

"I can't help it, Rebecca. It's because I'm deeply concerned about your safety."

"My safety? How absolutely gallant of you, Walter," she chuckled. "She's only a little girl, darling. I'll be perfectly fine."

"I still think it's the wrong decision. What possessed you to take her in?"

"I told you. I wanted an assistant."

"But then why choose this wretched slum urchin? I could easily have helped you find far better candidates. I would even gladly pay their salary for you."

"That's very sweet and generous of you, Walter. But I've made my decision. Little Bess will come live with me to be my maid and companion."

Bess opened her eyes upon hearing her name and looked up at Miss Sutcliffe, who smiled at her.

Mr Huxley cleared his throat. "Rebecca, if it's companionship you want–" He took her hand in his and gazed into her eyes. "You know my offer still stands."

"I do, darling." She smiled sweetly, even as she withdrew her hand from his. "But you know I like my freedom."

"Marriage needn't be akin to captivity," he chuckled, trying to make light of the situation.

"True. But only when you're a man. For a woman, a wedding ring soon proves to be the first shackle in a long and heavy chain that takes all the joy out of her life."

"Our marriage wouldn't be like that." His pleading voice sounded desperate. "I would give you everything your heart desires. A beautiful home, servants, dresses, jewellery. Even freedom."

He tried to take her hand again, but she deftly deflected his gesture and tenderly placed her hand on his cheek. "You're a sweetheart, Walter. But it could never work. One of us would inevitably end up being miserable." She smiled and lowered her hand again. "And besides, your mother would never approve of someone like me."

Just as he wanted to protest, the carriage came to a halt and she glanced outside. "This is where we get out, my little angel," she said to Bess.

They had stopped in front of a rather plain looking terraced house. But it was four storeys high and Bess tried to imagine how many rooms it had. She pointed and asked, "Is that your home?"

"Not all of it," Miss Sutcliffe chuckled. "But it's where I live. My room is on the top floor. It's very cosy." She took Bess by the hand and got out of the cab. "Thank you for the ride, Walter. Good night."

"Good night," he muttered from inside the carriage while pulling his coat a little closer around his chest.

"Wave goodbye to Mr Huxley, dear," Miss Sutcliffe told Bess sweetly. But the producer ignored the girl and gruffly knocked on the cab's ceiling to instruct the driver to be on their way.

"I don't think he likes me very much," Bess said as the carriage drove off.

"I think you're right," Miss Sutcliffe giggled. "Come on. Let's go inside."

Bess followed her up to the front door and waited while Miss Sutcliffe searched for her key.

"You'll have to be quiet," the actress said. "It's late and we don't want to wake anyone up. Especially not my landlady, Mrs Edwards."

Bess nodded gravely. Her heart started beating more quickly as she suddenly realised: she was going to sleep in a proper house again tonight! For years, she had been living on the street – sleeping in alleys, doorways and a variety of abandoned buildings. But those days were over now. She still couldn't believe her luck.

When they reached Miss Sutcliffe's room on the top floor, Bess entered with hesitant, shuffling feet.

"Welcome to your new home," the actress said while she lit an oil lamp.

Bess looked around and was surprised the room appeared to be so sparsely decorated. She saw a bed, a stove, a table with some chairs, a wardrobe and a sideboard with a small mirror standing on it. Somehow she had expected more.

"What do you think?" Miss Sutcliffe asked, taking off her hat and coat.

"It's... nice."

"Do I detect a hint of hesitation?" the actress smiled as she gracefully sat down on the bed.

"Oh no, Miss," Bess hastened to say. "It's much nicer than anywhere I've lived in years. And I didn't mean to sound ungrateful."

"But?"

Bess shrugged. "I'd have imagined someone like you would be living in a palace."

Rebecca laughed. "I'm afraid actresses don't make nearly as much money as you seem to think, dear." She got up and went over to the sideboard where Bess spotted a washbowl and a large pitcher.

"How about we give you a wash, so we can go to bed?"

Bess nodded and looked round again. "Where shall I sleep, Miss?"

"Why, with me of course."

"Oh no, Miss," she gasped. "I wouldn't dream of troubling you. I'll sleep on the floor. What I meant to ask was, where do you want me: in front of the stove, or on the rug next to your bed?"

"Don't be silly. Only animals sleep on the floor. You're sleeping in bed with me. Nice and snug. But that's why we need to get you washed first." She poured water in the washbowl and took a piece of soap. "Go on, take off those rags of yours."

Blushing, Bess undressed. Holding her threadbare clothes close to her, she asked, "Where shall I put these, Miss?"

"Just put them in a corner, dear. We'll throw them away in the morning."

"Throw them away?" She hugged her dirty rags even tighter. "Why? They're mine. And they're the only clothes I have."

"But they're practically falling apart, sweetheart. And they're rather smelly. If you're going to be my assistant, you will need nicer clothes. We'll go out and buy you some, first thing tomorrow morning."

Miss Sutcliffe gave her one of those mesmerisingly reassuring smiles and Bess relented. If she was to have a new life, throwing away her old clothes was as good a start as any, she supposed.

Next, she padded over to the sideboard and let the actress wash her. The water was cold, but the soap was lovely. It smelled of flowers and it made her skin feel soft.

When they were done, Bess stared at her arms and legs in amazement. "I'm so pale!"

Rebecca giggled. "That's because you're clean. Look at all the filth and grime that's come off."

She pointed at the washbowl and Bess wrinkled her nose in disgust at the pitch-black water.

"I'll give you one of my nightshirts to wear," Miss Sutcliffe said, going over to her wardrobe. They both changed, but the nightdress Bess put on was so ridiculously big for her, the sight caused the two of them to burst out laughing.

"Oh dear, we really do need to get you new clothes in the morning," the actress chuckled as she wiped the tears from her eyes. "Let's quickly go to sleep. We've got a busy day tomorrow."

She turned down the oil lamp until the flame went out, and then slid into bed. "Come," she said, beckoning to Bess.

The young girl climbed in beside her, with a mixture of excitement and trepidation. Once they were tucked in, Rebecca snuggled up close behind Bess and placed a sweet little kiss on her ear.

"Good night, darling," she whispered.

"Good night, Miss."

Bess wasn't sure if she would be able to sleep. It was all so new and so hard to believe. But the warm, cosy weight of the blankets and Rebecca's soft breathing soon got the better of her.

I hope I'm not dreaming this. I hope I won't wake up in that miserable old factory in the morning.

But even if it was only a dream, then it would still be the best one she had ever had.

Chapter Eight

The sound of a milkman's cart rattling through the street roused Bess from a deep slumber. She opened her eyes and blinked a couple of times, taking in the unfamiliar surroundings as the faint grey light of early morning began to chase the shadows from the room.

So it wasn't a dream, she sighed in relief. She sat up straight in bed and stretched. Lying beside her, Miss Sutcliffe appeared to be still asleep. Bess studied her peaceful face. *So pretty,* she thought. How could anyone as beautiful and talented as her be living in a small and modest room like this?

A very cold room too, Bess realised as the icy chill in the air made her shiver. She hopped out of bed, went over to the stove on her bare feet and got a fire going.

"I see you're taking your duties very seriously," a husky voice said from behind her, startling her slightly. Bess spun round and saw Miss Sutcliffe smiling at her.

"It was very cold in the room, Miss. So I lit the stove. I hope you don't mind?"

"Of course not. Saves me the trouble of having to get out of this wonderfully warm bed."

Encouraged by having done the right thing, Bess asked, "What would you like me to do next, Miss?"

"I want you to come back to bed, so we can have a snuggle while we wait for the room to warm up."

Bess was more than glad to oblige and slipped under the blankets again. Rebecca let out a little shriek when she felt the girl's cold feet against her legs.

"Your feet are freezing," the actress gasped. "Luckily, I know just the thing to warm you up."

Before Bess could say anything, Rebecca started tickling her, making her laugh and giggle. Being a maid was getting better by the minute, it seemed.

When they lay quietly for a moment to catch their breaths, Bess' stomach suddenly made a rumbling noise, sending them into another laughing fit.

"Have you hidden an angry monster underneath these blankets?" Rebecca teased. "Or are you hungry?"

"There's no monster, Miss," Bess chuckled. "It's just my tummy."

"Well, I suppose you'd better rustle up some breakfast then. You'll find eggs, bread and cheese in the cupboard."

Eager to please and impress her mistress, Bess jumped out of bed and prepared a simple breakfast in record time.

"You seem perfectly at home here already," Rebecca commented as she lazily slipped on a dressing gown and came over to the table. "And you've even brewed a pot of tea. Well done, my angel."

Beaming with pride, Bess filled the first cup and watched as Rebecca breathed in its rich scent with her eyes closed.

"Simply divine," the actress sighed. "Just the thing I need in the morning."

"I hope you'll like the eggs as well, Miss. I'm afraid I'm not very good at cooking."

"Don't worry, dear. You can't possibly be any worse than me, because I must be the most horrible cook in the world."

She winked and Bess covered her mouth as she giggled. Just when they wanted to tuck into their breakfast, there was a rather urgent sounding knock at the door.

"That will be Mrs Edwards, the landlady," Rebecca said, answering Bess' startled look. She got up and opened the door.

"Good morning, Mrs E. I had a feeling you would be coming round." Rebecca sounded overly delighted to see the slight woman, who seemed bad-tempered and unfriendly to Bess.

"Morning, Miss Sutcliffe," the landlady replied, her thin lips crunched up in a perpetually dour pout. "I thought I heard laughter and voices. So I wanted to check what all the commotion was about." She looked rather short, but there was nothing sweet or innocent about her, Bess felt. Because Mrs Edwards' eyes shone darkly with menace.

"Commotion, Mrs E? I trust we haven't caused any nuisance to the other tenants?"

"If you have, they didn't mention it to me. Not yet anyway. But since you are usually not in the habit of rising before noon, Miss Sutcliffe, I felt it wise to investigate the source of your apparent mirth."

The landlady eyed Bess with suspicion. But Rebecca deliberately put off introducing her new maid a bit longer.

"In case I had brought a visitor into my room last night, you mean, Mrs E?" she said teasingly. "A male visitor perhaps?"

The landlady turned a deep shade of red and wagged a finger at her tenant. "Don't you put any words in my mouth that I didn't utter, Miss Sutcliffe! I trust you to know the rules of this house."

She spoke the last sentence while staring hard at Bess, clearly annoyed that Rebecca wasn't getting the hint and still hadn't explained the presence of this girl sitting at the table.

"Of course, Mrs E," Rebecca answered sweetly. "I wouldn't dream of causing a scandal under your roof." She smiled at her landlady for a moment and then pretended to remember something. "Oh, please allow me to introduce my new assistant to you. This is Miss Morgan and she will be helping me with a variety of tasks."

The surly pout returned to Mrs Edwards' lips. "A bit young, isn't she?"

"They're cheaper that way," Rebecca said. But she turned to Bess and winked with a cheeky smile as soon as she had said it. "Besides, Bess has already proven that she's perfectly capable of alleviating the practical burdens of my busy life."

Mrs Edwards snorted mockingly. "You must be so relieved, Miss Sutcliffe." She smoothed down her skirts and inspected the room with a probing look. "As long as the waif keeps quiet and doesn't damage any of my property, it's fine with me. Although of course," –a greedy smile made the corners of her mouth curl up– "you understand this means I shall be obliged to raise your rent. Your lease was agreed for one person, not two."

"But of course, Mrs E," Rebecca nodded sweetly. "I wouldn't have expected anything less from you."

The landlady shot Rebecca a vicious glare at the barely hidden insult. "Speaking of which, you'll kindly remember next month's rent is due in less than a week."

"I hadn't forgotten, Mrs E. How could I, since you always remind me several times?"

"I merely like my tenants to pay on time, Miss Sutcliffe. That is all. I will let you know the surcharge for this extra tenant by the end of today."

"That will be perfectly in order, Mrs E. Oh, and might I ask a small favour of you?"

"A favour, Miss Sutcliffe?"

"Could we borrow a set of children's clothing from you? I'm afraid Miss Morgan has suffered a small wardrobe malfunction and we'll need to dash to the market this morning. But she can hardly venture outside wearing nought but my nightshirt."

"Hasn't got any other clothes, has she? Where did you find the waif, Miss Sutcliffe? In the gutter?" Mrs Edwards chuckled with a mean little snigger.

Refusing to take the bait, Rebecca merely continued to smile amiably. "We'll pay you for your trouble obviously. And we'll return the clothes to you as soon as possible – washed and folded, naturally."

"Naturally, Miss Sutcliffe. I'll bring up some clothes for the girl later and I'll add the charge to your rent."

"Much obliged, Mrs E."

"I shall leave you to your breakfast now." She began to turn back, but then paused. "Oh, and Miss Sutcliffe?"

"Yes, Mrs E?"

"I trust you won't be taking in any more street urchins? This is a boarding house, you know, not an orphanage."

"Very droll, Mrs E," Rebecca laughed. "But I can assure you I will only be needing one assistant."

She closed the door behind her landlady and returned to the table.

"I'm sorry," Bess said, lowering her head.

"What for, darling?" Rebecca asked as she sat down.

"For causing you trouble with your landlady."

"Oh, that." She gave a short dismissive wave with her elegant hand. "Don't worry about it, dear. Mrs E is one of those people who enjoy being difficult. But as long as the rent gets paid on time, she isn't too much of a bother."

"Why do you call her Mrs E?"

"Because I know she hates it," Rebecca grinned. They both giggled mischievously. Their breakfast had turned cold in the meantime, but Bess didn't care. Miss Sutcliffe was the best and most exciting thing that had ever happened to her!

Chapter Nine

"Did we really have to throw away my old clothes?" Bess asked plaintively as their hired hansom cab slowly made its way through the busy city traffic. She was wearing the hand-me-downs Mrs Edwards had lent them. They weren't quite her size and they had been mended a few times in several places. But at least they were nicer than what she used to wear.

Miss Sutcliffe chuckled, "Were you that attached to those tattered old rags, my darling?"

"No," Bess replied hesitantly, although she had to admit her current clothes felt uncomfortably unfamiliar to her. "But we should have sold them instead."

"I doubt anyone would have been willing to give us more than a few pennies for them, dear. Why would we go through that much trouble for so little money?"

Bess nodded. *I have a lot to learn,* she thought. Miss Sutcliffe might have claimed that actresses didn't make a lot of money, but to Bess' eyes, she was wealthy. Why else would her mistress insist on taking a private cab instead of an omnibus?

"Yes, the omnibus is cheaper," Miss Sutcliffe had told her. "But they're awfully crowded and some of the passengers can be rather uncouth. Girls like us should travel in style, dear."

Bess had to admit there was some truth to it. Since the driver of this sort of carriage sat behind them at the top, they could look out over the back of the horse – affording them an unobstructed view of the street while they rode.

"I almost feel like a princess," she blushed and giggled.

"Just you wait until we buy you a few new outfits," Miss Sutcliffe said. "Then you'll even start looking like a princess." She squeezed Bess' hand and giggled as well.

"Please remind me, Miss: what's the place called we're going to?"

"Petticoat Lane market, dear. They've got more clothes there than you can shake a stick at. It's said that if you're looking for a piece of clothing – anything at all– and you can't find it at Petticoat Lane? Why, then it simply doesn't exist. But even that isn't a problem, because you can simply walk into any of the dressmaker shops in the area and have it made for you."

Bess gazed out dreamily in front of her, trying to picture what it was going to be like – to stroll around at the market like a proper young lady.

"Speaking of dressmakers," Miss Sutcliffe continued. "We'll have to visit mine next week."

"Do you need a new dress, Miss?"

"Ladies are always in need of new dresses, dear," the actress laughed. "But I meant for you. We'll go see my dressmaker so she can make something nice for you."

Bess gasped. "You want to have a brand new dress made for me?"

"Of course, dear. We'll only find the basic necessities at the market – decent and fairly new things, mind you; not like this old, patched up stuff Mrs E gave us. But you need something truly lovely as well. Something made to measure just for you."

Bess didn't know what to say. She had never owned a dress like that before. "Are you sure, Miss?"

Rebecca smiled. "I can't have my assistant looking like a street urchin, can I? And besides, you'll need a pretty dress for opening night."

When their cab arrived at the edge of the market, Rebecca paid the driver and then the two of them began their great adventure. Because that's exactly what it felt like to Bess: a thrilling, grand adventure.

Miss Sutcliffe was very convincing as a well-to-do middle-class lady out shopping with her young daughter, for whom she only wanted the best.

"If I tell them you're my maid," the actress whispered to Bess, "then they're sure to fleece us. They would try to sell us poor quality rubbish. And we don't want that, do we?"

She winked and Bess had to cover her mouth with her hand to stop herself from giggling. This was even better than she had imagined. The stallholders were quick to spot a well-heeled patron like Miss Sutcliffe and eagerly called out to her. Sensing there was good money to be made, they bent over backwards to please their customer.

In less than two hours, she had purchased more clothes for Bess than some people would own in their entire lives. It was too much for them to carry, so Miss Sutcliffe paid a man to deliver it to her lodgings.

"When he arrives on our doorstep with all of that, I'm certain Mrs E will turn green with envy," she laughed.

But Bess was beginning to feel tired and drained. Shopping was more exhausting than she had thought.

"Are you hungry, dear?" Miss Sutcliffe asked.

"Just a little bit," Bess nodded. "There's a man selling sausage rolls over there. Could we have one, please?"

"Certainly, dear. But wouldn't you rather have a proper luncheon?"

Bess wasn't sure what constituted a proper lunch. To her, a sausage roll used to be a full meal; something she and Nan would only be able to afford when they had the money. Which wasn't often.

"I–" She stared at her feet and fumbled with her dress, feeling ashamed and frustrated about how little she knew of the world. "I don't know what you mean, Miss."

"Then you'll find out soon enough, my darling," Miss Sutcliffe smiled. She took a big shiny coin from her purse and handed it to Bess. "Here, buy yourself a sausage roll first. That'll tidy you over until we get to Pierre's."

"Thank you, Miss," she said, accepting the coin. "Who's Pierre?"

"It's the name of the restaurant where I'm taking you to lunch, sweetheart."

"What's a restaurant?" she asked, fearing Miss Sutcliffe must think her very stupid indeed.

But her mistress merely smiled that kind and patient smile of hers. "You'll see when we get there. Now go grab a sausage roll before they're sold out."

Half an hour later they stepped out of another cab and into an establishment that, according to Miss Sutcliffe, was one of the nicest places to have lunch. A finely dressed gentleman with a delicately combed moustache and a rigidly straight back stood inside near the entrance.

"Miss Sutcliffe," he greeted her. "What an absolute pleasure to see you again. Table for two?"

As he escorted them to their table in the restaurant, Bess had to keep herself from staring with an open mouth. The place looked like a palace to her. People in fancy clothes sat at individual tables enjoying their meals while talking politely. Everything was so clean and... civilised.

Bess felt horribly out of place. *People are bound to see right through me,* her anxious mind said. Despite her new clothes, they'd know she was nothing but a wretched street rat. And then someone would demand that she leave immediately.

But nothing of the sort happened. Instead, when they reached their table, a waiter came over and pulled back her chair for her while the gentleman with the fine moustache did the same for Miss Sutcliffe. Unsure what to do, she shot a panicked look at her mistress, who smiled reassuringly and gestured at her to sit down.

"Today's menu," the gentleman said, handing them each a large sheet of paper with fancy scribbles on it. "Our special this afternoon is glazed duck à l'orange. Enjoy and please let me know if there's anything you need."

He bowed stiffly and returned to his post by the door.

Blushing, Bess leaned over to Miss Sutcliffe and whispered, "What does it say, Miss? This... menu, the man called it? I can't read, you see."

"That reminds me we'll need to find someone who can teach you to read and write."

"I'm sorry," Bess said, lowering her head in shame.

"No need to apologise, sweetheart. These things don't come naturally to anyone, you know. We all need to learn." Once more, Miss Sutcliffe treated Bess to one of those kind smiles of hers – a smile that made you feel good about yourself.

"The menu shows you what you can order in this restaurant," she explained. "We tell the waiter what we want and then someone in the kitchen will make it for us."

Bess nodded and stared at the scribbly letters again. They still didn't make any sense to her, but suddenly she felt an eagerness to learn and understand what the words meant.

"It looks like there's a lot on this menu," she said.

"And all of it is equally delicious, I can assure you."

"I bet it's expensive," she whispered as she eyed their posh surroundings.

"Very expensive," Miss Sutcliffe replied matter-of-factly.

Bess gasped in shock. "But then why are we eating here? That sausage roll back at the market was all the lunch I needed."

"A sausage roll is nothing but a snack, my dear," the actress chuckled. "A young girl like you needs to have a proper meal."

"But you're making me feel guilty, Miss."

"Guilty? What in heaven's name for?"

"Because you've already spent so much money on clothes for me. And now we're eating in this fancy place. You won't have any money left."

Miss Sutcliffe gently placed her elegant hand over Bess' much smaller hand. A big red gemstone glittered magnificently in the ring on her finger. "Bess, my dear," she smiled. "You needn't worry about money anymore. Those days are over for you."

"I just don't want you to get in any trouble because of me, Miss. You said yourself that actresses don't make nearly as much as I thought."

"I appreciate your concern, my little darling. And it's awfully sweet of you. But money is useless if we don't spend it."

"As long as you're sure you've got enough, Miss."

"Some would say there's never enough money, darling," Miss Sutcliffe replied with a smile. But it was a strange smile. Because for the first time, Bess thought she detected a hint of sadness on Miss Sutcliffe's face. The dark cloud passed quickly however, expertly driven away by a talented and experienced actress.

Chapter Ten

The tip of Bess' tongue was sticking out slightly at the corner of her mouth as she put away the last of the dinner plates in the cupboard, her movements slow and careful so she wouldn't break anything.

"I've finished with the washing up for the evening, Miss," she said, looking over to her mistress. The actress was sitting in front of the small mirror on the sideboard that also served as a dressing table.

"Well done, dear. You are the most excellent assistant."

Comments like that still made Bess glow with pride, even if they were said half-jokingly. She smoothed down her apron – one of the many things they had bought at the market the week before – and came to stand closer to Miss Sutcliffe.

"Is that makeup you're putting on?"

"That's right, sweetheart."

Fascinated, Bess watched while Rebecca put the finishing touches to her toilet. Miss Sutcliffe was the first woman she knew who used powders and lotions and creams on her face. Not that she needed any of it, in Bess' opinion.

"Why do you use makeup, Miss, when you're already as beautiful as you are?"

"You know, it's the funniest thing," Miss Sutcliffe smiled. "Wearing makeup is frowned upon by so-called polite society. But men always expect a woman to look her absolute best. So we have to help nature along with discreet and artful interventions. The trick is to enhance your features without drawing attention to the makeup."

Next, Miss Sutcliffe took her favourite bottle of expensive perfume and applied some of it on her neck and the top of her dress. It smelled of flowers and things Bess didn't recognise.

"How do I look?" she asked, turning to Bess, who gaped at her in fond adoration.

"You look gorgeous, Miss. You always do." Wistfully, she added, "I wish I could be half as pretty as you are when I grow up. But that will never happen."

"Oh, darling. Beauty and elegance aren't like a gift or a natural talent you're born with. Sure, some people may have a head start in life when it comes to their looks. But it's much more about knowing how to dress, how to talk and how to conduct yourself in company so that men admire you, and other women envy you."

"Could you teach me?"

Smiling, Miss Sutcliffe planted a kiss on Bess' forehead. "I'll tell you all my little secrets when you're a bit older, my darling."

She got up and took her handbag. "I must be going now. I've told you I'm seeing someone important tonight and it wouldn't do to keep them waiting."

Miss Sutcliffe stepped towards the door.

"You won't be afraid, will you? I hate to leave you alone in our room like this, but there's no other way."

"I'll be fine, Miss. I've got some more tidying up to do and then I'm going to practise my sewing. Mrs Roberts has been showing me the basics."

"Mrs Roberts is a sweetheart – and probably the best seamstress in the theatre. So you listen carefully to what she tells you, all right?"

"I intend to, Miss."

"Good girl," the actress nodded as she finally opened the door and stepped onto the landing. "I'll close and lock the door, but you've got a spare key, remember?"

"Yes, Miss."

"Don't wait up for me. Because I probably shan't be home until very late. Good night, my darling."

"Good night, Miss."

Standing in the middle of their small room, Bess watched as Miss Sutcliffe closed the door. She heard the key turning in the lock, followed by the fading sound of footsteps descending the stairs. Soon, silence was her only companion in the room and she let her eyes drift around for a moment.

Our room, Miss Sutcliffe had called it.

Not her room; *our* room. It was a small and seemingly insignificant word, but it made a huge difference to Bess. Because it meant this was her home too now.

She smiled to herself when she remembered how disappointed she had been the first time she laid eyes on it – expecting Miss Sutcliffe to be living in some sort of palace, instead of this modest single room on the top floor of a perfectly ordinary house. But at least it was cosy and Bess would do her best to make it look even better.

After she had done all the tidying up that she could think of, she rewarded herself with a nice cup of hot cocoa – another one of those divine delicacies that she had discovered thanks to Miss Sutcliffe.

With her nose hovering over the steaming cup, she breathed in the rich aroma and let out a blissful sigh of delight. To make the pleasure last longer, she drank her cocoa slowly.

But as soon as she had drained the last delicious sip, she washed up her cup and neatly put it away. There would be no mess when Miss Sutcliffe returned. Then she took out her sewing and sat down at the table, determined to make both Mrs Roberts and her mistress proud.

Eventually, after a few hours, her eyes grew tired and so she decided to call it a night. Having changed into her nightshirt, she turned down the light and went to bed.

Lying on her back with her eyes open, she wondered what Miss Sutcliffe was doing. Would she still be talking to the important people she was meeting? Or would she be on her way back home by now? Miss Sutcliffe had warned Bess these sort of appointments usually went on until very late at night. And that sometimes she only got back when the first light of early morning began to show in the sky.

Fancy chatting to someone for that long, Bess thought. *I'm sure I'd fall asleep halfway through.* Grown-ups could be so strange.

Yawning, she rolled to her side. And as she felt her mind drifting off, her last thoughts before falling asleep were of the breakfast she would prepare for her mistress and herself in the morning. Miss Sutcliffe was bound to be hungry after a long night like that.

She didn't know if she had been sleeping for only a short while or a few hours when she woke to the sound of someone shuffling about in the dark.

"Miss?" she whispered drowsily. "Is that you?"

"Did I wake you, my darling?" Miss Sutcliffe's familiar voice came back softly. "I'm sorry. I tried to be as quiet as possible." Bess thought the actress sounded exhausted.

In the faint moonlight that shone through the thin curtains, she could see the shape of her mistress slipping out of her clothes and coming over to the bed. When Miss Sutcliffe lifted the covers and snuck into bed, a rush of cold air made Bess squirm. Quickly, they both snuggled up to each other for warmth and comfort.

But as they did, an unpleasant odour penetrated Bess' nose. "Now who's the smelly one?" she complained, remembering when their roles had been reversed.

"So sorry, dear. It's because I've been in a place where most people were smoking and drinking. I'm afraid we'll have to air my dress for a while in the morning. Tobacco smoke always clings to your clothes." Miss Sutcliffe's voice was rapidly becoming weaker and sleepier.

"Why would anyone want to smoke tobacco if it makes your clothes smell so horrible?"

"People do the oddest things unfortunately, sweetie." When she hugged Bess closer to her, there was a curious intensity to her embrace.

"Miss?"

The sleepy reply only came after a short pause. "Yes, dear?"

"Are you sad, Miss?"

"Just tired, darling. Let's go to sleep now, please."

Bess listened to the soft sound of Miss Sutcliffe's breathing as it slowed down and turned into the steady rhythm of a deep sleep. But even as she too began to fall asleep again, there was a feeling she couldn't get rid of. She was sure she had heard sadness in her mistress' voice.

And she wondered what someone as sweet and lovely as Miss Sutcliffe could be sad about?

Chapter Eleven

When the stage curtains closed, an ecstatic roar went up throughout the theatre – so loud Bess had to cover her ears. Everyone in the audience jumped to their feet, cheering and applauding like mad. Shouts of 'encore' went up and people were calling out Miss Sutcliffe's name.

The curtains slid open again, revealing the cast members who were standing on stage in a neat row. Rebecca, obviously, had been given the centre spot. As the actors took their bows, the thunderous applause showed no sign of dying down.

This had to be repeated a few more times, until Miss Sutcliffe found herself standing alone in front of the closed curtains, gratefully accepting the continued cheers and shouts that were aimed exclusively at her. Several people brought her flowers and when she wiped away her tears of joy, people seemed to clap even louder.

Bess figured everyone's hands had to be raw from clapping them together so hard and for so long. But she too was beaming with pride and happiness. The new play was a tremendous success!

Once Miss Sutcliffe had waved a final goodbye to the crowd and disappeared behind the curtains, Bess made her way backstage, where everyone was visibly as excited as the audience had been. She wanted to go over to her mistress, but she quickly changed her mind when she saw how many people were swarming around the triumphant actress.

Most of them were men, she noticed. They all wanted to congratulate the undisputed star of the evening and exchange a few words. Each single one of them was vying for her attention, while Mr Huxley appeared to be glued to her – jealously keeping guard over *his* actress.

"Look at all those silly peacocks," Mrs Roberts chuckled when she appeared by Bess' side. "Strutting their stuff and fawning over the hen with the golden eggs." The seamstress rolled her eyes. "Men are such predictable creatures."

Bess gave a wry smile, pleased to hear someone else shared her own impression of the scene before them.

"That's another reason why I admire your mistress so much, you know," Mrs Roberts said. "The way she can keep smiling at those dreadful fools. Me, I wouldn't have the strength nor the patience for it."

Nodding silently, Bess studied Miss Sutcliffe's face. There was something about that smile, she thought. It seemed graceful and charming as always, but it wasn't the same sort of smile Bess got to see when they were alone. If she had been older, she might have recognised the difference: there was no genuine love in this smile.

"Miss Sutcliffe is a very good actress," she said.

"She most certainly is, my love," Mrs Roberts agreed. "She's the best I've seen in a very long time. And that's saying something, because I've been a seamstress in this theatre and many others for over twenty years."

They fell silent for a brief spell during which they both stared at Miss Sutcliffe as she stood surrounded by her chattering admirers. She seemed like a goddess to Bess – perfect, graceful and completely in control.

Bess heard Mrs Roberts letting out what sounded like a sad sigh. She frowned and looked up, but the seamstress merely flashed a quick smile in response.

"How's your sewing coming along, dear?"

"Quite well," Bess answered happily. "Thanks to you of course, Mrs Roberts. Miss Sutcliffe says I'm learning from the best."

"Oh, shush," the seamstress waved with a modest blush on her cheeks. "Have you had much chance to practise lately, what with the preparations for opening night and all?"

"It's true we've been busy these past few weeks. But I always try to do a bit of sewing every day."

"Miss Sutcliffe must be very pleased to have such a devoted and eager assistant."

"She says I'm doing great. But sometimes I think she just says that to make me feel good."

"If that's what you think, then I believe you're being too hard on yourself, dear," Mrs Roberts smiled. "And I hear you're learning to read and write now as well?"

Bess nodded vigorously. "Miss Sutcliffe has found an excellent teacher for me. And she's said that, in time, she'll let me write her letters for her."

"That's what assistants do, isn't it? Oh hello, here she comes now. Rebecca, darling!"

The actress had finally managed to extract herself from her pack of admirers and came over to Bess and Mrs Roberts. Giddy with glory, it looked as if she was walking on air.

"Isn't it fabulous, my darlings? People really seem to have liked the play."

"The play was all right," Mrs Roberts said. "It's you they adored, dear."

"Yes, you were magnificent, Miss," Bess added.

"Did you think so, my angel? Oh, I'm so happy to hear it. Walter says he's extremely pleased as well."

"He should be," Mrs Roberts snorted. "That man doesn't deserve you."

Miss Sutcliffe squatted down in front of Bess. "Listen, my darling. We're all going out to celebrate in a bit. So go fetch our shawls in the dressing room, if you please."

"Do you think that's wise, love?" Mrs Roberts asked. "Doesn't seem like the sort of thing for a girl as young as her."

"But I want to come along," Bess protested. "I want to celebrate your success as well."

Miss Sutcliffe hesitated and looked at Mrs Roberts for guidance.

"It's bound to get terribly late, dear," the seamstress said to Bess. "And girls your age need their sleep." She turned to Miss Sutcliffe and asked, resolutely, "Shall I walk her home for you?"

The actress stood up again and bit her lip. "If you wouldn't mind awfully? Oh, you're such a dear, Mrs Roberts."

Bess wanted to argue, but the matter already appeared to have been decided.

"I don't want you to walk that far though," Rebecca said. "Especially not at this time of day. I'll give you some money for a cab. No, no, I insist."

A short while later, Bess was on her way home in a hired hansom cab, with Mrs Roberts sitting beside her. Although she understood the reasoning behind the decision, she was still sulking about not being allowed to join in the celebration with the others.

"Most generous of your mistress to let us ride home in a carriage," Mrs Roberts said, more cheerfully than was needed.

"She's always like that," Bess replied, letting out a sigh. She realised Mrs Roberts had only wanted to help, so it wouldn't be fair to be grumpy with her. "Miss Sutcliffe says money doesn't make you happy unless you spend it and share it with others."

"True! Why, I daresay that someone who buys a hearty pie with their last pennies and shares it with a friend will have more joy in their lives than one of those tightfisted old misers sitting on a fortune."

Mrs Roberts continued to chat away about a variety of everyday things, which had the welcome effect of lifting Bess' mood.

"We're nearly there, I believe," the seamstress said. "Will you be all right on your own? Or would you like me to come up with you?"

"Oh, there's no need to worry, Mrs Roberts," Bess replied confidently. "I'm used to being alone in the evenings by now. Miss Sutcliffe often has appointments she needs to go to, you see. Several times a week even. And they usually last until very late at night, so she can't take me with her."

"I see," Mrs Roberts said, looking straight ahead.

"To be fair though, I don't think she likes them very much, you know, these appointments."

"And why is that, dear?"

"Just a feeling," Bess shrugged. "Most of the time, she seems terribly tired afterwards. A little bit sad even. Still, Miss Sutcliffe says it helps to pay the rent."

"Of course."

"Although I don't understand how," Bess frowned. "How can a rendezvous– that's what Miss Sutcliffe calls it; it's a French word, did you know that? Sounds very fancy to me. Anyway, I don't see how a rendezvous would help to pay the rent. All it is, apparently, is people talking and smoking and drinking for a very long time."

"How old are you, Bess?"

"Eight. But I'll be nine soon."

Mrs Roberts nodded and vaguely stared into the distance somewhere ahead of them.

"Do you think," Bess started asking hesitantly, "that perhaps, with this new play being a success and all, things might change?"

"How do you mean, dear?"

"If lots of people want to see the play, they all need to buy a ticket. And then maybe Miss Sutcliffe won't need to go on so many of these late appointments."

The cab pulled up in front of Mrs Edwards' lodging house and came to a halt. Mrs Roberts gave Bess a painful look and gently stroked the girl's hair. "Let's hope so, my darling. Are you sure you don't want me to come up with you for a little while?"

Bess shook her head and got out of the cab. "No, I'm fine, thank you. And thank you for taking me home, Mrs Edwards. Good night."

"Good night, love. And try not to worry too much about Miss Sutcliffe. She's strong and she's a smart woman, I'm sure."

As they waved to each other and the carriage drove off, Bess thought Mrs Roberts looked at her with sadness and pity in her eyes.

Maybe the seamstress was disappointed because she too had wanted to celebrate with the others? Grown-ups could be so confusing.

By the time she got to their room on the top floor, Bess felt too tired for a cup of hot cocoa, so she went straight to bed.

When she woke up the next morning, Miss Sutcliffe was lying next to her, fast asleep. Quietly, Bess slipped from underneath the blankets and decided to air her mistress' clothes, as she was sure they would be smelling of tobacco smoke and other unpleasantness again.

Chapter Twelve

"Dear Miss Sutcliffe, I simply had to take my pen in hand to congratulate you on your captivating performance in your latest play, The Queen of Nazaria."

Bess looked up from the letter she was reading to Rebecca. "He even spelled it right."

"Impressive," the actress chuckled, lying on her back on the bed while she slowly inspected her nails.

"The way you breathed life into this fictional character was most convincing," Bess continued reading out loud. "And the passion you brought to the stage succeeded in rousing my heart."

"Oh dear," Rebecca said with a hint of mischief in her voice.

"Wait, there's more," Bess giggled. "Even today, on the morning after I had the privileged pleasure of watching you perform, I find myself distracted and thinking about your stunning appearance. Please consider me an ardent admirer of your talent, who is looking forward to your next production impatiently. Yours devotedly, Henry T. Morris, Esq."

Putting down the letter, Bess inhaled deeply to catch her breath from this gentleman's impassioned outpouring.

"Goodness me," Rebecca smiled affectionately. "Put him on the pile of people who get a nice reply. I think Mr Morris has earned a few kind words of gratitude, don't you?"

"He sure has," Bess nodded. "A lovely thank you note – with a charming reminder to encourage all his friends to go and see the play."

"Obviously," Rebecca quipped.

A double knock sounded at their door, and Bess instinctively turned her head towards it.

"That'll be good old Mrs E," Rebecca sighed. "Perhaps we've been giggling too loud to her liking again."

Bess got up and went to open the door.

"Good morning, Mrs Edwards," she said with a beaming smile. At twelve years old, Bess was already taller than their short-statured and notoriously disagreeable landlady. Just to emphasise the big difference in their character, Bess always made an effort to be extra polite to Mrs E.

"These arrived for you from the theatre," the landlady grumbled. "More letters. A messenger boy has just delivered them."

Exuding an air of immense disdain, she handed over another stack of envelopes to Bess, holding them as if they were something foul and despicable.

"Oh, thank you, Mrs Edwards! Most kind of you to bring them up to our room."

"Yes, I wouldn't usually of course," came the snooty reply. "But I feel it makes for such a horribly cluttered mess having all these letters lying about in the downstairs hallway. As you know, Miss Morgan, I'm rather fond of order and neatness in my house."

"I'm terribly sorry for the inconvenience," Bess smiled warmly. "But as you may have heard, Miss Sutcliffe's latest play is once more a tremendous success."

"I think I have glanced over a newspaper report or two that alluded to the matter," the landlady said. She tried to make it sound as if the whole affair didn't interest her in the slightest.

But Bess heard the jealous undertone and she could easily picture Mrs E sitting at her kitchen table, bitterly grinding her teeth as she pored over every word of the ecstatic reviews heaping lavish praise on Miss Sutcliffe.

"She's been on a bit of a winning streak these past few years, hasn't she?" Mrs Edwards smirked. "Must be nice to be able to pay the rent on time."

"It most certainly is, Mrs E," Bess replied fondly, taking pleasure in using the pet name they knew their landlady hated. "Thank you once again for bringing up these letters."

She swiftly closed the door and went back to the table, putting the fresh batch of mail with the rest.

"Did dear old Mrs E strike you as a tad envious?" Rebecca asked with a mocking grin.

"Just a little bit, yes," Bess joked. They shared a guilty giggle and then Rebecca came over to the table as well. She picked up a letter in each hand and cast a twinkling eye over the words.

Brushing aside a lock of loose hair, Bess said, "I'd better get started on writing your replies. It seems you're sent more letters with each successful play."

"I know. If this trend continues, we'll have to move to bigger lodgings just to accommodate the growing amount of post," Rebecca jested.

"But we could never do that, Rebecca! We'd miss good old Mrs E too much."

They snorted with laughter and Rebecca picked up another handful of letters. "Oh, hello," the actress said. "Listen to this one." She began to stride through the small room while she read the letter out loud, enunciating its contents as if they were the words of a play by Shakespeare.

"My dearest Miss Sutcliffe, I have had the immense pleasure of witnessing you play the role of The Queen of Nazaria only last week. Since that time, my mind has been haunted by the memory of your mesmerising performance every waking moment of the day."

She looked up from the letter and told Bess, "I hope he's not going to complain about losing sleep because of me."

"At first," she went on reading, "I attempted to ignore this heightened emotional state of mine, thinking it would be of a passing nature; merely the result, as it were, of my deep appreciation of your artistically beautiful portrayal."

"However–" Rebecca paused and her eyes widened in surprise as she saw the next part of the letter. Suppressing a smile, she cleared her throat and pressed on.

"However, after long and careful consideration, I have come to the conclusion that this is no temporary infatuation. I would therefore be so bold and daring as to ask for your hand in marriage."

"What?" Bess gasped, not knowing if it was better to be shocked or amused by this. "Surely, he's jesting?"

Rebecca quickly scanned the rest of the letter and shook her head. "No, he seems absolutely serious about it. He even wants me to meet him for tea at The Alexandra next Thursday at two o'clock in the afternoon. Oh, and he assures me he is a man of substantial means, perfectly capable of providing me with the opulent lifestyle I rightfully deserve."

"Are you going to accept his invitation to tea?"

"Most certainly not! Men who are that love-struck usually turn out to be dreadfully boring. The fire of their passion burns brightly for a brief moment, but then all you're left with is ashes and dust."

With a sigh, she tossed the letter back on the table. "Besides, I have Walter to consider. The poor darling would have a seizure and drop dead from pure envy if he found out I had tea with a mysterious suitor."

Bess tried to grin at the mention of Mr Huxley. Even after several years, she and the theatrical producer still hadn't warmed to each other. The dislike was, and would remain, entirely mutual.

"Speaking of whom," Rebecca said, gazing at the pile of letters on the table, "I wonder which one of these is actually from Walter posing as an admirer."

"Why would he do that?" Bess frowned.

"To get a kind reply from me. A few sweet words of thanks, scribbled gracefully on paper scented with a whiff of my perfume."

"But–" Bess was virtually speechless. This was one of the most bizarre things she'd ever heard. Far more bizarre than some of these love letters they received. "But Rebecca, I'm the one who writes your replies. Surely, he'd notice the difference in handwriting?"

"Not Walter Huxley, dear. The silly old fool is far too gullible to notice. As long as it looks pretty and dainty and the letter smells nice? He'll cherish it as a priceless treasure."

Fingering leisurely through the pile of letters, she said, "If there's one in here asking for a lock of my hair or something silly like that, then you may rest assured it's from Walter. He would do anything to get his hands on a little souvenir from me."

Bess shook her head warily. In her imagination, she could see the delighted producer sniffing the scented letter and pressing it to his heart. The thought made her wrinkle her nose in disgust.

Rebecca strolled over to the bed and let herself fall on her back, with much theatrical grace and a profound sigh. "Men can be such a queer and tiresome sort," she said.

"Do you think you'll ever want to marry one?"

"I'm not sure I'll ever find one who would want to marry me. You forget I'm an actress, sweetie. No decent man in his right mind would dare to risk his reputation by marrying an actress."

"Mr Huxley would marry you. He's said so on several occasions."

"Walter is more like a doting uncle, dear," Rebecca chuckled. "He isn't marriage material. Not much of a man either, to be frank. Did you know he still lives with his mother? Besides–" She got up from the bed again and spun around on her feet, with her arms spread out like a pair of wings. "I think I prefer my freedom. Men may claim they adore my plucky spirit, but as a husband I'm sure they'd rather pluck my feathers and put me in a gilded cage."

Bess grinned. She felt quite certain there wasn't a cage in the world strong enough to hold the spirit of Rebecca Sutcliffe.

Chapter Thirteen

Perfect, Bess thought. Having inspected her neat row of stitches, she was pleased with the result. Her hand reached for the mug of tea standing close by on the dining table, but she found it empty.

"Time to put another kettle on then," she announced. It was just her in the room, since Rebecca had gone out on one of her late night appointments. But after six years of being Rebecca's assistant, Bess had grown quite used to spending these evenings on her own. Between cleaning, washing, sewing, reading and writing letters, she was never at a loss for things to do.

She got up and stretched her back, detecting a slight stiffness. *Must have been sitting for longer than I realised,* she decided. *Tell you what, I'll run down to the hallway to see if there's been any post this evening.* Taking the stairs from their room on the top floor and back would give her the bit of exercise her sore limbs needed.

She had just picked up the few letters that were lying on the side table in the hallway, when she caught her reflection in the mirror hanging on the wall. Smiling, she admired the new dress Rebecca had bought her the week before. It was plain yet elegant, and Bess remembered glowing with pride the first time she had tried it on at the dressmaker's. Standing before the mirror in Mrs Edwards' hallway, she did a little twirl to get a better glimpse of the back of the dress.

"My, my," a familiar sounding snarky voice said, startling Bess. "How pretty you look."

"Oh, good evening, Mrs E," Bess said, quickly recovering her wits but still blushing. "I didn't hear you coming down the stairs."

Reaching the bottom step, the landlady glared darkly at Bess. "Are you implying I'm sneaking around in my own house, Miss Morgan?"

"I wasn't implying anything, Mrs E," Bess pointed out. *Although we all know lurking about and eavesdropping are two of your favourite pastimes, you wicked old bat,* she added silently.

"No, you were admiring your fancy new dress in my mirror, weren't you?" Grinning unkindly, Mrs Edwards approached Bess and touched the folds of the dress to feel the fabric. "Very pretty indeed."

"Thank you," Bess said uncomfortably, moving away half a step. "I'm glad to hear you like it too."

"Must have cost a fair sum of money. Another gift from your mistress, I take it?"

"Yes, Miss Sutcliffe is very generous like that."

"I suppose you could call it generosity, yes," the landlady smirked. "Others might be more inclined to think of it as being a spendthrift."

"How others judge my mistress is their choice," Bess answered pointedly, as she tried to head for the stairs. She had a bad feeling their landlady was in the mood to stir up all sorts of nastiness, so she wanted to be as far away from her as possible.

But Mrs Edwards wasn't going to let the opportunity escape her that easily. "Judging by the quality and finish of your fine dress," she said quickly as Bess reached the bottom steps of the stairs, "I'd hazard to say the money could probably pay for several weeks of rent."

Bess stopped and took a deep breath. Was Mrs Edwards simply trying to pry the price of the dress from her? Or was there more to it than that?

"We always pay our rent on time, Mrs E. You know that. Or are you now the one trying to imply things?"

Take that, you mean old fruitcake.

"Remarkable, isn't it?" the landlady said with an overconfident grin. "The way your mistress never fails to pay her rent, while still having plenty of money to maintain such a grand lifestyle?" Assuming an air of contrived innocence, she added, "I mean, after all, she's only an actress."

"A very successful actress, Mrs E," Bess reminded her defiantly. She didn't see where this conversation was leading to. But wherever it was, she didn't like it.

"Oh, I know, dear," Mrs Edwards continued sweetly. "Miss Sutcliffe is a woman of many talents. But still–" Drawing out the moment, she ran a finger over the edge of the side table, checking it for dust.

"One sometimes wonders where she gets the money from. Actresses don't exactly earn a lot. Not even the more successful ones." She nodded in Bess' direction with a smile, as if to acknowledge the last point.

"Surely, as her trusted maid and faithful assistant, you must have some idea of the level of Miss Sutcliffe's income from her theatrical life? Have you never wondered how she can afford these gifts and all this so-called generosity?"

Bess shook her head. What business was it of Mrs Edwards –or anyone else– to know how much money Miss Sutcliffe made? Or how she paid for things? But privately, Bess had to admit the question did cross her mind from time to time.

"Oh, come now, Miss Morgan. You may not be a woman yet, but you're a clever girl, aren't you?" A malicious sparkle twinkled darkly in Mrs Edwards' eyes.

An inner voice screamed at Bess to stop listening and hurry up the stairs. But she felt trapped in the web of intrigue that Mrs Edwards had cunningly spun for her. As she watched the landlady taking a step towards her, much like a sinister spider crawling closer to its helpless prey, Bess' breathing was becoming quicker and more shallow.

"You have a fine pair of eyes to help you see, haven't you, Miss Morgan? And a sharp mind to think? So don't tell me you haven't figured it out yet."

"Figured out what?" Bess had to force herself not to tremble with fear as their landlady came to stand awkwardly close to her.

"Why, the connection of course," Mrs Edwards whispered with a sense of glee as dark as a moonless night. "The connection between your mistress' seemingly carefree finances... and those mysterious late-night appointments of hers?"

"I–" Bess swallowed, her throat suddenly feeling parched. "I don't know what you mean."

"Then let me spell it out for you, Miss Morgan. Your mistress is a courtesan. Wealthy gentlemen give her money and expensive gifts in return for her companionship at their clubs and other places that are conveniently removed from the public eye."

Bess stared at Mrs Edwards in silent horror. She was unable to utter a single sound, feeling as if someone had knocked the wind out of her.

"Oh, I'm sorry," the vicious landlady smiled angelically. "You seem somewhat surprised. Almost as if this information is completely new to you."

Bess wanted to howl in agony and lash out at this cold-blooded, ugly monster before her. The words Mrs Edwards had spoken were like an evil claw that had reached deep inside her chest and ripped out her warm, pulsating heart.

But all she could manage was to run up the stairs and dart into their room, while tears streamed freely down her face. She threw herself onto the bed and cried herself to sleep.

Chapter Fourteen

She woke up with a start when she heard the key turning in the lock. Rebecca was back! Bess immediately sat up straight in bed, unsure what time of night it was.

Expecting her to be fast asleep, Rebecca gave her a startled look. "Bess? Did I wake you up, darling?" Then she noticed the burning oil lamp and asked, worriedly, "Why is the light still on? And why are you wearing all your clothes? Are you unwell, sweetheart?"

She hurried over to the bed and sat down on the edge, putting one hand on Bess' forehead. "You haven't got a temperature, have you?"

Bess shook her head and drew back – not much, but enough for Rebecca to notice.

"What's the matter, my darling? Oh Bess, you've been crying," she said when she spotted her red and swollen eyes. "What happened? Did you hurt yourself?"

She scanned the room for any signs of an accident. Finding none, she turned back to Bess and looked at her with a concerned and pleading gaze.

"Mrs Edwards," Bess merely said, fighting back a fresh batch of bitter tears.

"What about her?" Rebecca gasped, her senses on high alert. "What did that horrid little goat do to you?"

"She told me."

"Told you what, my darling? You're not making sense, sweetie. Did you take a tumble and knock your head?"

"She told me about you. And where you go to in the evenings."

"Oh," Rebecca replied flatly. "I see."

"She said you're a– what did she call it? A courtesan!" The words began to rush forth from her, the pain and hurt still feeling raw and real. "She said you let rich men pay you to keep them company at their clubs. And that's how you manage to afford to live the way we do."

"Bess–" Rebecca gently placed a slender, graceful hand over Bess' hands, which were clutching at the bed sheets.

"Is it true, Rebecca? Please say it isn't so!"

Rebecca regarded her with a painful expression on her face. "I'm afraid it's true, my precious darling."

"No-o-o," Bess wailed as she threw herself into Rebecca's open arms. She buried her face in the chest of the one person she had adored more than anyone else in the world. Overcome by a seemingly never-ending stream of tears and sobs, she held onto the woman who had seemed so perfect to her. So faultless.

Rebecca waited and tenderly stroked Bess' hair, until the crying gradually subsided. Once she felt a bit calmer, Bess laid down, with her legs pulled up and her head resting in Rebecca's lap.

"How did it get started? You becoming a courtesan, I mean?" She wasn't sure if Rebecca would be willing to tell her about it, but Bess wanted to know.

"Well, I never went looking for it and I never meant it to happen," Rebecca replied in that soft and velvety voice of hers. "You could say the thing sort of happened to me."

"Tell me, please."

"Years ago, long before you and I met, a married lady friend took me along to this posh soirée with lots of rich and important people. I was introduced to several of the other guests, including a distinguished gentleman. His name doesn't matter anymore now."

She frowned and continued, "And to be frank, I'm not even sure I remember who it was exactly. There have been so many names and so many faces over the years. But he was kind, and very charming. That evening, we merely talked. About art, current affairs, life. The next morning, he sent me flowers and a note inviting me to a private dinner."

"And is that when he asked you to be his courtesan?" The word still sounded strange and exotic to her ears.

"No, men never ask, darling. These matters are... understood – silently. They're never spoken out loud. You talk, you laugh, you share a drink. And then the gentleman merely assumes the lady knows what's expected of her. It wouldn't do for their pride and their self-esteem to plainly state their intentions."

"I don't think I understand."

"Neither did I – at first." Rebecca sighed. "I was young and very foolish. For a while, I believed he actually loved me. But these men don't want love. They want a devoted companion: a pretty playmate who panders to their ego and their sense of self-worth."

"Haven't they got a wife who can do that for them?" Bess asked naively. "If they're wealthy and important, then they shouldn't have any trouble finding suitable marriage candidates."

"Oh, they're married all right. Very respectably too. But that's not what it's about. Having a companion is different. They know they are in complete control of the relationship. They hold all the cards."

Rebecca's face hardened as she added, "This control, this power they hold over another human being – that's what they're really paying for. The companionship is merely a happy consequence of the arrangement."

"It doesn't sound like a very nice experience to me. Not for you as their companion anyway."

"Believe me, it isn't, sweetheart."

"But then why do you continue doing it?"

Rebecca grinned wryly. "I've asked myself that question a few times. And the honest truth is I don't really know. I suppose the money is part of the reason why. I'd be quite poor without the extra income. And it's nice to be able to buy lovely things and surround yourself with a dash of comfort and beauty. Makes life more enjoyable."

"Is that all? Doesn't seem worth it to me somehow."

"No, you're right." Rebecca paused and hesitated briefly. "I've often wondered, and it shames me to say this, but... I think part of me secretly enjoys the attention. It's flattering in a strange sort of way. Especially since most people look down on actresses. Even these fine gentlemen would pretend to scorn me in public. Privately however, behind closed doors—"

A voluptuous smile took hold of Rebecca's lips. "To not merely be admired, but to be desired with such intensity... It's thrilling and terrifying at the same time."

With her head still resting in Rebecca's lap, Bess could feel the shudder that ran through the actress' body.

"So there," Rebecca said. "Now you know my greatest, darkest secret: I'm a courtesan. Gentlemen pay me for a few hours of sophisticated entertainment and discreet companionship."

"Why didn't you tell me sooner?"

"I meant to, sweetheart. But you seemed so happy. So innocent. I didn't want to ruin that. I was afraid that the weight of my secret would crush your carefree heart. And so I kept putting it off, always thinking I could wait a little longer to tell you."

Rebecca hung her head and sighed, "I realise now it was wrong of me to do that. You deserved to hear the truth from me, instead of from the vile mouth of that scheming serpent."

"Yes, I would have preferred that as well. Hearing it from Mrs Edwards, and in such a mean, deliberate way... It gave me a nasty shock. I wanted the world to end."

"I'm so sorry. Bess. You have every right to hate me. And if you no longer want to live with me, I understand."

"Rebecca–" Bess sat up and looked at her imploringly.

"I can ask around to see if any decent families are looking for a maid. Not just any old household maid of course. You'd make an excellent lady's maid. Or maybe Mrs Roberts would want to take you on as an apprentice. You know, in case you'd rather become a seamstress?"

"Rebecca, please," Bess interrupted. "I don't want to leave you."

"You don't?" Rebecca asked, staring at her incredulously. "But you know now who I am. Don't you despise me for that?"

"You are who you've always been to me: Miss Rebecca Sutcliffe – not just a great actress, but more importantly, a wonderful person with a heart of gold. The woman who took me in and gave me a life when I had nothing."

119

With tears of joy coming to her eyes, Bess hugged herself close to her mistress. "I love you, Rebecca."

"I love you too, my darling," came the teary reply. "You have no idea how much I love you." Raining tender kisses and happy tears on Bess' head, she added, "I've never really thought of you as my maid, you know. You've always been my little girl. Right from the start when I saw that wide-eyed, dirty little face of yours."

They laughed at the memory, through tear-filled eyes and runny noses.

"I guess this means you and I have something in common," Bess said, relieved to put this horrible episode behind them. "We both did what we had to do in order to survive." She chuckled. "Although entertaining rich gentlemen probably doesn't make you as dirty as living on the street does."

Rebecca tried to smile. "Perhaps," she replied sadly. "But it'll kill you in the end just the same."

Chapter Fifteen

A lethargic groan emanated from the bed, while Bess busied herself with tea and breakfast over at their small stove. "Good morning, Rebecca," she said, doing her best to sound upbeat and perky. "Your eggs will be ready any minute. And I've made your tea extra strong. I figured you could do with some double-strength brew this morning."

Another muffled groan was the only response she got. Glancing over her shoulder, she saw Rebecca rolling onto her back in bed. When the water boiled, she poured it over the ample supply of crushed tea leaves in the teapot.

Bringing it over to the table, she chuckled, "Here you go. One pot of life-restoring dark brew, ready and waiting for you. Guaranteed to work like magic."

Forcing herself to get out of bed, Rebecca listlessly dragged her feet as she joined Bess at the dining table. "I appreciate you're trying to cheer me up, darling. But please save yourself the effort. I've made up my mind to feel thoroughly miserable today."

Bess slid the fried eggs onto a plate with buttered toast and placed it in front of her sorrowful looking mistress, who decided she wasn't hungry and politely pushed the eggs away. "You have them, sweetheart. Tea will do me nicely, thank you."

Pouring the tea, Bess wasn't willing to give up on the happy tone just yet. "After breakfast, I'll pop downstairs to see if there have been any more letters. Then we can go over them together and think about what to write back."

She sat down and watched as Rebecca stirred three spoonfuls of sugar into her cup.

"There won't be any letters, darling. Bills maybe. But no letters. Not with the current catastrophe." Rebecca sipped her tea and pulled a face in disgust. "Too sweet."

"Would you rather have coffee?" Bess asked, desperate to please. She hated seeing her mistress this gloomy.

"No, don't bother."

"It's no bother. Really," she said, moving to get up and make coffee.

"Sit down, darling," Rebecca urged. She attempted to smile at Bess, but the gesture didn't quite reach her eyes and seemed hollow as a result. "I'm just being difficult, sweetheart. That's all. I'll drink the tea, don't worry." She took another sip and winced at the sickly sugariness of it.

"Are you sure you don't want to eat something?" Bess nodded encouragingly at the eggs and toast.

Rebecca shook her head, bravely hazarded some more tea and asked, "Have you seen the morning papers yet?"

"Y-yes..." Bess replied hesitantly.

"And?"

"Nothing interesting really. The usual nonsense about crime and politics and such."

"You mean they didn't even bother to write about the play?"

"Well, yes. They did. But–" She let the words trail off, hoping in vain to evade the matter.

"But what? What did they say, Bess? It can't have been anything favourable. People absolutely hate the play. Yesterday, someone snored –rather loudly, I might add– throughout my entire tragic monologue."

"The reviews I've seen are nothing but vicious jealousy and hateful slander."

"Read them to me."

"Rebecca, I don't think we should–"

"I'm a grown-up woman, Bess. Theatre critics may be beastly monsters, but I've known men far worse than them. Now read me those reviews or pass me the papers and I'll read them myself."

Bess relented and went to fetch the newspapers she had tactfully hidden from sight. But before she opened them, she cast a reluctant frown at Rebecca. "You're sure?"

"Positively certain." She placed her teacup at her lips and braced herself, staring hard in front of her. "Skip the boring parts and only give me the juiciest bits."

Turning to the arts section, Bess cleared her throat and began, "Rebecca Sutcliffe's latest production, 'The Flower Girl of Church Lane', is billed – somewhat generously – as a family drama. But in this reviewer's most humble opinion, the word 'disaster' would be a more fitting description."

"There may have been a time when Miss Sutcliffe was considered (undoubtedly by less discerning members of the public) to be a rising star in the arena of British theatre."

"However, it would now seem that our star has come crashing down to Earth. Or that, in keeping with the flower girl theme of the play, the rose has lost its former lustre and has begun to wilt and wither. Let us pray that the blossom of yesteryear will not spread obnoxious fumes as she slips further into decay."

Bess paused and looked up from the paper, bristling, "They must think they're very witty writing such garbage."

"Keep reading, sweetie," Rebecca said, before taking a sip from her tea. Her eyes were fixed on an indeterminate point on the far wall.

"We kindly remind our readers that 'The Flower Girl of Church Lane' isn't Miss Sutcliffe's first brush with failure. Previously, 'The Princess of Babylon' only met with moderate success, whereas 'The Orphan of Strawberry Street' was an outright fiasco that, according to reliable sources, nearly bankrupted the theatre where it was performed."

"In conclusion (and it pains us to say this) we cannot help but wonder whether Miss Sutcliffe, who once showed a tiny glimmer of promise, has proven herself to be past her prime already?"

Rebecca calmly finished her tea, while her placid face seemed like a mask of cool indifference.

Feeling compelled to fill the uneasy silence, Bess put the papers down with an offended huff.

"Journalists, they call themselves," she grumbled. "Cowards, is what I say they are. Sitting behind their desks, spreading such lies and venom in their sleazy columns. How dare they strike at their victims like that? Don't they realise how hurtful their words can be?"

"Oh, they know all too well, darling," Rebecca said impassively. "It gives them pleasure."

"What a wicked thing to do! It's wrong, it's indecent, and it's–"

"It's also true," Rebecca interrupted her. "There's no denying the play is a frightful flop. Ticket sales are slow, to say the least, and the theatre is likely to shut it down soon. Which is probably for the best." Languidly, she rose from her seat and stepped away from the table.

"Doesn't it trouble you?" Bess asked.

"What, darling? The scathing reviews or the failing play?"

"Both, I guess."

"Fame and fortune are such fickle things," Rebecca shrugged. "They come and they go." Moving to the mirror on the sideboard, she stroked the side of her face and studied her reflection. "Perhaps the newspapers are right. Maybe my best days are behind me. Certainly my looks are beginning to fade."

"That's not true and you know it," Bess blurted out forcefully. "You're still an amazing actress and you're as beautiful as ever."

"Thank you, darling," Rebecca smiled as she came over to Bess and caressed her hair. "You always say the nicest things, my lovely angel. Don't ever change." She bent over and placed a tender kiss on the girl's cheek.

"Come," she said, her mood instantly bright and cheerful, as she took Bess by the hand and pulled her to her feet. "We shouldn't sulk and sit around in this dingy room. Let's go for a stroll along Regent Street. And then we will enjoy an extravagant meal someplace insanely expensive."

Bess laughed nervously. She was happy to see this sudden change of temperament, but also concerned about the likely financial consequences.

"I'm all for a walk in the fresh air, Rebecca. But do you think it's wise to go out and spend money on frivolous things, given our current circumstances?"

"Oh, hosh-posh, darling," Rebecca replied, dismissively waving her hand in the air. "It's absolutely vital that we maintain a joyful spirit of abundance. *Especially* under our current circumstances."

She skipped over to their wardrobe and started rummaging through it. "Come on. Put on your most colourful attire. I command it."

With her eyes wide in childlike excitement and a sparkling smile that was impossible to resist, she threw Bess a brightly coloured shawl.

Diving back into the wardrobe, she added, as if it was the most normal statement, "We'll pop round to the pawnbroker's shop on our way to town and sell a piece of jewellery."

Chapter Sixteen

Carrying the wrapped up dress she had collected for Rebecca at the dressmaker's, Bess was feeling gloomy. High above her head, a bright summer sun marched radiantly across a clear blue sky. But she had too much on her mind to notice. Lately, their money problems had only grown deeper, although Rebecca usually didn't seem nearly as concerned as Bess.

They had become regular customers of the pawnbroker's, as they had fallen into the alarming habit of needing to sell something valuable once or twice every month. But this too didn't appear to worry Rebecca. Her gentlemen supporters were always showering her with expensive gifts and jewellery, she claimed.

"Plenty more where that came from," she would joke to Bess each time the next piece was sent off to their favoured pawnbroker, Mr Sullivan.

Bess, however, wasn't so sure. She had noticed for instance that Rebecca wasn't wearing some of her favourite rings anymore, suspecting that they had been sold off.

And neither had it escaped her attention that her mistress had been staying in more often in the evenings. When Bess had casually remarked on the change, Rebecca had laughed and said she preferred spending a quiet night at home with her over having to entertain inebriated rich men with questionable morals. But she knew the real reason was simply because Rebecca had been securing less appointments.

And yet, despite these troubling signs, Rebecca hadn't curbed her liberal spending habits. No amount of arguing, pleading or protesting from Bess could temper her mistress' urge to keep their wardrobe in line with the latest fashion or to go out for sumptuous meals in exclusive places. Rebecca seemed insatiable in her desire to spend money.

Bess had begun to lose sleep over it as their financial situation grew more precarious. The decline was slow, for now, but she was under no illusion about where it would end. On more occasions than she cared to count, she had found herself lying awake in bed at night, fretting over how to turn the tide.

Not once though did she blame Rebecca. She simply couldn't find it in her heart to do that. Not because she was foolish or naive. But rather because she believed she had caught glimpses of the sadder, tortured side of her mistress' fragile soul.

They hardly ever talked about such matters, and Rebecca went through much trouble to show the world her confident and optimistic side. But Bess knew better. She had witnessed the rare unguarded moments, when hints of heartache and sorrow would come shining through.

Deeply lost in this festering swill of dark and burdensome thoughts, Bess was completely oblivious to the bustling foot traffic on the high street she was navigating.

That is, until she accidentally knocked into a gentleman.

"Can't you mind where you're going, you blithering idiot?" he grumbled while he stooped to pick up his hat.

"I'm terribly sorry, sir," she said, her voice trembling with nerves. *Thank goodness Rebecca's dress is unharmed,* she thought.

"The Lord has given you a pair of eyes for a reason, you know," the man complained, dusting off his hat. "So I suggest you use them."

"I will, sir. Please accept my apologies. Good day to you, sir." She turned round, intent on getting away from him before he made too much of a fuss.

But in her haste, she promptly ran into another pedestrian: a large and heavily perspiring man. Bouncing into his enormous belly nearly sent her, and Rebecca's precious dress, crashing to the ground.

"What the devil," the large man swore hotly.

"The child must be a simpleton, sir," the first man said. "She has just done the same to me."

An elderly gentleman joined them. "Today's youth don't know any manners, that's the problem." Angrily, he waved his cane at her. "She might even be a thief, creating a diversion. Check your pockets, good sirs."

"It was merely an accident," Bess muttered. "A thousand pardons, sirs." She nodded her head and quickly took her leave, pressing the new dress close to her.

In her anxious mind, every single person on the pavement suddenly turned into a potential threat. And as her jittery heart began to race, her eyes darted towards the road where a multitude of carts and carriages clattered along. If one of them drove through a muddy puddle or a pile of steaming manure just as it passed her, the dress would be ruined!

I need to get away from the busy high street, she decided. Turning into the first side street she came across, she soon found herself cutting through passages, alleys and smaller backstreets.

Just like old times, she grinned, reminiscing about her previous life as a child of the slums. She wasn't overly familiar with her present surroundings, but she felt confident she could rely on her natural instincts to find her way through the maze of narrow and winding streets. After all, she told herself bravely, she had grown up in a brutal world of filth and cobblestones, very much like the one she was plodding through now.

The deeper she penetrated this city wilderness however, the more she sensed her guard going up. People were staring at her. To their eyes, she was a young lady from an entirely different class.

A fearful voice in her head began to question the wisdom of taking the route she had chosen. And when a barrage of cruel laughter echoed off the crooked walls around her, it made her hair stand on end.

"Look what we have here, lads," a sarcastic voice said. "It's a princess." More laughter sounded.

"Wandered straight out of a fairy tale, she must have. Lost your way, princess?"

Footsteps came rushing towards her, as three youths ran up to her and blocked her way. She was trapped.

"Need any help?" the one in the middle asked, grinning at her from underneath an unruly mop of ginger hair. "We're perfect gentlemen, we are. And we're more than happy to oblige a pretty thing like yourself."

He gave one of the other lads a playful shove of the elbow and they all sniggered. Bess tried not to look at their faces, her panicked eyes searching for an escape instead.

The ginger leader studied her more closely, cocked his head at a funny angle and said, "Well, I'll be–" He poked her shoulder with his finger. "Oi, remember me? I'm your old friend Freckle Face. Or are you too good for the likes of us now?"

Bess stared at him in surprise and then the penny dropped for her too.

"Joe?" He was much taller now obviously – almost a man in fact. But she could still see in him the boy he had once been. The boy who had taken her stolen pie from her, only to save her from the police the next day.

"So you do remember me," he grinned. "I was afraid you wouldn't recognise me this far away from our old haunts. You're not the only one who's been moving up in the world, you know."

Bess thought his present slum territory didn't seem like much of an improvement over the previous one. But she knew better than to tell him that.

"What brings you here, pretty princess?"

"I'm running an errand for my mistress." Now that she knew the leader of this small pack of street thugs, her initial fears were calming down a bit. And a rebellious sense of defiance was beginning to take its place.

"Turning into quite the young lady, aren't you?" Joe said, eyeing her up and down.

She decided to ignore his remark and stuck her chin out. "I need to be on my way."

"Why the hurry? Haven't you got a bit of time to spare for an old friend?"

She had half a mind to wipe that stupid grin off his face. But the constant brainless sniggering of his accomplices at his every remark was even more infuriating.

"No, I haven't," she said haughtily. "And we were never friends to begin with."

"Feisty. What have you got there, princess?" He reached out a grubby hand, but she instantly slapped it away.

"Keep your filthy paws away from Rebecca's new dress," she hissed.

"A dress, is it?"

"Yes, and it's brand new. I've just picked it up from the dressmaker's." She blurted it out without thinking, vaguely hoping it would impress them. If she could convince them that her errand was important, then perhaps they would let her go. Or so she foolishly reasoned.

But that wasn't how Joe's mind worked.

"Tailor-made, eh? Must have cost your mistress a pretty penny. Maybe we should take it from you and sell it," he sneered. "I like the feel of big coins in my pocket."

"Don't you dare," Bess growled, narrowing her eyes. Rebecca would be devastated if she heard someone had stolen her dress. And then she would more than likely order a new one, making their financial pain even worse.

"Don't be silly, princess," Joe scoffed. "You don't stand a chance against the three of us."

"Oh, really?" Now it was her turn to smirk, while old memories and survival instincts came rushing back to her. "I seem to remember we've been in this sort of situation before," she said, baring her teeth to remind him of the time she bit his hand to defend what was hers.

The tiniest flicker of alarm flashed in his eye, but then he grinned at her and said, "Tell you what. I'll let you walk away – with your precious dress – if... you give me a kiss."

"What?!"

But Bess wasn't the only one who didn't like his proposal. Joe's associates grumbled too. "Blackfoot won't like it when he hears we let a prize like this get away."

"Yeah, Joe. That dress is worth a lot of money."

Joe's lip curled up in an angry snarl. "Then I guess Blackfoot won't be hearing about this, will he?"

"But Joe–"

A quick punch to the gut put an end to the objection.

"Blackfoot is getting on in years, lads. I may not be the only one to have my eye on the top spot, but I'm a lot smarter than all the others."

"Yes, you are, Joe," the other lad agreed, eager to avoid getting punched like his friend.

"So we're clear on this? Blackfoot doesn't need to know we ran into a pretty little princess with a fancy dress today."

"Whatever you say, Joe," the first lad grunted, rubbing his painful belly.

"Wonderful. Now–" He turned back to Bess. "How about that kiss?"

"Never!"

"Suit yourself," Joe shrugged. "We'll take that dress then." He tried to grab her parcel, and when Bess pulled it away from him, he grabbed her by the arm.

"It's very simple, princess. The dress, or a kiss: what'll it be?"

Bess was shaking with anger at the unfairness and utter disgrace of his proposal, but she realised the answer was obvious.

"I'll kiss you," she said, her voice barely louder than a whisper. "But I swear I won't like it," she added resentfully.

"You won't know until you've tried," he teased as he turned his head towards her and tapped the side of his face.

Squeezing her eyes shut, she leaned in reluctantly to kiss his unshaven cheek. But at the very last moment, he shifted his head slightly and kissed her full on the lips. Her eyes snapped open in shock and she pulled back, horrified and flushing with shame.

Joe grinned brazenly while his friends roared with laughter. "See how her cheeks have turned red, lads? That means she loved it. Maybe I should ask her for another one, eh?"

"You said I could go if I gave you a kiss," she fumed, anger briskly replacing her embarrassment. "I've fulfilled my part of our agreement, now you hold up your end of the bargain."

"Only joking, Your Highness. I told you I was a gentleman, didn't I? And a gentleman keeps his word." Stepping aside, he gave a respectful wave with his arm to let her pass. "You're free to go."

She took one tentative step towards freedom, suspicious about any traps or further nonsense. But when he merely smiled at her, she dashed past him and ran off.

"Feel free to visit us again anytime though," he called after her mockingly, much to the audible amusement of his friends.

Hurrying back to the high street, she cursed herself for making this detour. Bess felt deeply ashamed of what she had done. But she'd had no other choice. She had done it to save Rebecca's dress.

When she emerged once again onto safer streets, she slowed her step and forced her breathing and her heartbeat to relax. But the sense of guilt and humiliation lingered. And she wondered if this was how Rebecca felt every time she had to entertain one of her gentlemen for an evening.

Chapter Seventeen

Forced to travel at a snail's pace, the hansom cab crept through the hectic late-morning traffic. The driver shouted abuse at every cart that half-blocked the road while being unloaded. And he seemed particularly adept at flinging choice words at the drivers of slow-moving omnibuses.

"I don't know what's more vexing," Rebecca sighed. "How long it's taking us to get to the train station, or this driver and his vulgar tongue."

"Don't worry," Bess replied. "We'll make it to the station in time."

"I hope so. It simply won't do to be late. That would be awfully rude to poor Phineas. This being his first time in London and all that."

They had received a polite letter from Rebecca's nephew, informing his aunt that he had obtained a position as a clerk in the City – courtesy of his father's relations. And that he would be arriving on the 11.55 train at the Great Eastern Railway terminus station on Thursday in two weeks' time. Which was today.

"Just think how disappointed the boy will be when he steps off that train and doesn't see us waiting for him. He'll feel decidedly abandoned in all that chaos on the platform." She rapped on the roof of the cab. "Hurry up, driver! We can't let my nephew down."

"Doing the best I can, m'lady," the driver said gruffly, immediately following up his reply with another shouted insult at a carter who wasn't moving fast enough to his liking.

"Calm down, Rebecca," Bess smiled. Seeing her mistress this nervous was a rare sight indeed.

"I don't even know if I'll recognise him. I haven't seen Phineas in ages."

Although Bess knew Rebecca was prone to exaggerate, in this case she was inclined to believe her. Because in the twelve years that she had been Rebecca's maid, her mistress had never paid a visit to her only sister. The odd distant letter once every few years was the only form of contact the two sisters seemed to have.

"Beatrice doesn't approve of my life and the choices I've made, you know," Rebecca said, rightly guessing Bess' mind. "We're very different that way, she and I. My sister has always been the sensible one. I guess that's why she married Edward."

Bess nodded silently, sensing that this was a more delicate and painful topic than Rebecca cared to admit.

"Don't get me wrong," her mistress continued. "Edward is a decent man. And rather well-to-do obviously, which is why Beatrice married him in the first place. But he's so terribly dull."

Bess grinned as she tried to picture Beatrice: a docile woman sharing Rebecca's family roots and physical features, she imagined, living a meek existence as an obedient wife and devoted mother.

"Phineas was their firstborn and he absolutely worshipped me when he was a little boy," Rebecca reminisced with a smile. "He was such tremendous fun."

She paused and a sad frown came over her face. "But then, shortly before the christening of her third child, Beatrice came all the way to London just to tell me, quite bluntly, that she preferred if I stopped visiting them."

Bess let out a disapproving hiss. "That's awful. Why would she do such a thing?"

"Too ashamed of her eccentric actress sister. Said their friends and neighbours were beginning to gossip, and that she had her husband's reputation to think of."

Rebecca smiled weakly at Bess, betraying how much the incident must have hurt her. "I hope she hasn't succeeded completely in destroying the poor boy's spirit."

Just then, the train station came into view and Rebecca instantly turned into her familiar vivacious self again. She grabbed some coins from her purse, so they could pay the driver more quickly.

"Oh, and Bess," she smiled. "Let's not mention my special gentlemen friends to Phineas just yet. He's probably perfectly sweet and innocent. We don't want to alienate the poor darling straight away."

"Of course," Bess replied earnestly.

As soon as the cab stopped, Rebecca thrust the fare through the hatch in the ceiling while urging the driver to release the door. Walking faster than what was deemed appropriate for a lady, they hurried to the platform where Phineas' train had just arrived. Clouds of steam drifted over the sea of passengers who were to-ing and fro-ing throughout the busy station.

"There he is," Rebecca exclaimed when she spotted her nephew in the throng of people. "Phineas, darling!"

She darted over to a young man holding a carpet bag in one hand and a large travel case in his other.

"Aunt Rebecca!" His face lit up with joy – pure and unmistakably genuine. The first thing Bess noticed about him was that he shared his aunt's graceful looks. He even had the same intense green eyes.

Rebecca took hold of his arms and pressed her cheek against his on each side, by way of a fond welcoming kiss. Beaming with pleasure, she turned to Bess next and introduced them to each other. "Phin, please meet my wonderful assistant, Bess Morgan. Bess, this is Phineas Parker, the most adorable nephew in the whole wide world."

Bess held out her hand a bit awkwardly. She barely dared to look at his face, but his handshake felt strong and confident.

"Pleased to make your acquaintance, Mr Parker."

"I assure you the pleasure is all mine, Miss Morgan."

Having dispensed with the formalities, Rebecca cut in again, gushing with excitement. "Oh Phineas, darling. How you've grown! Why, the last time we met, you were a scrawny boy in breeches.

And look at you now: a handsome, strapping young man. Don't you agree, Bess?"

Trying in vain to keep herself from blushing, all Bess could manage was a nod of the head. She knew her mistress was doing it on purpose, to tease her – and enjoying it too.

He'll think I'm some sort of imbecile if I don't say something more intelligible soon, she admonished herself. But that only caused her face to turn a deeper shade of red.

"Are you hungry, Phin?" Rebecca asked. "You must be dying for a spot of lunch. Young men are always ravenous."

"As a matter of fact–"

"Right then," Rebecca said confidently, not even waiting for him to finish his reply, as she turned round and headed for the exit. "Follow me, my darlings. There's a delightful little place nearby. None of this nasty train station buffet rubbish."

"Mother warned me about your bohemian ways," Phineas chuckled. "Trust your aunt to know all the fanciest places to dine, she said."

"I'm so glad to hear my precious sister hasn't stopped thinking highly of me," Rebecca answered with a heavy hint of sarcasm. "Does she still roll her eyes as much whenever she talks about me?"

The amused grin on his face told Bess that Phineas appreciated his flamboyant aunt and her forthright style. Which made him even more likeable.

"And how is my dearest Beatrice?" Rebecca asked her nephew once they were seated at their table.

"Probably still the same as when you last saw her, Aunt. Mother never changes much."

"No, I suppose she doesn't. Predictability has always been one of her strong points."

"I'll say," he chuckled. Bess loved the wrinkle that appeared in his cheeks when he laughed. "Constance and Victoria are both fine as well. Although you probably wouldn't recognise them now."

"I'm sure I wouldn't. They were still so little last time. Victoria hadn't even been christened yet."

"They've certainly grown a bit since then. Such a shame you never seemed able to visit."

"I know, darling. Frightfully busy, you know," Rebecca lied for his sake, hiding the nasty truth behind one of her charming smiles. "And now you've come to work and live in London, your letter said!"

"That's right. Father arranged it all of course. He's even offered to pay for my rented accommodation for the first three months."

"Why London, dear?" Rebecca asked. "Not that I mind, obviously." She grinned and gave his arm a playful squeeze. "But I would have thought your mother would have wanted you to have a position closer to home?"

He leaned in and lowered his voice. "Don't tell Mother and Father, but my real reason is I want to become a playwright."

Rebecca let out an ecstatic shriek that turned a few heads in the restaurant. "My dear boy!"

Phineas smiled, visibly pleased his aunt approved of his idea. "My plan is to earn a regular income as a clerk, while I write plays in the evenings and in my spare time. Hopefully, I'll be able to turn it into a full-time profession in a few years. And maybe I'll try to write art reviews for the newspapers to make some more money. So you see, London is the place to be for me."

"Artistic *and* sensible," Rebecca quipped. Bess grinned, but her mind immediately drifted to their own money problems.

"Perhaps I could write a play for you, Aunt?"

Bess gripped her napkin as a painful silence fell over their table. Phineas looked at them both, frowning.

"That's very kind of you, darling," Rebecca smiled sedately. "But to tell you the truth–" She sighed. "I haven't had a successful play in years and nobody seems to be offering me decent roles anymore."

"Temporary setbacks happen," he said cheerfully.

"I'm afraid we've passed the temporary phase," Rebecca confessed. "It's been so long, I can't remember what a cheering audience sounds like."

Phineas looked shocked and turned to Bess, as if he was hoping she would tell him his aunt was only joking. But Bess shook her head and stared at her hands.

"I'm so sorry to hear that, Aunt. It was my understanding you were doing rather well for yourself."

"*C'est la vie,* as they say in French, darling. But let us talk of happier things now. Our lovely Miss Morgan here is celebrating her 20th birthday in three weeks."

"Congratulations," Phineas said cordially as if they were best friends already.

"You simply must join us, Phin," Rebecca insisted. "I wanted to throw a big birthday bash, but Bess isn't that sort of girl, I'm afraid. So we're settling on something more intimate."

Bess laughed. "And by 'intimate' your aunt means an à la carte dinner at The Café Royal."

"Nice and cosy," Rebecca nodded.

"I'll be more than happy to help you celebrate," Phineas said. When he smiled at her, Bess could have sworn she felt butterflies fluttering about in her belly.

Chapter Eighteen

Wearing her finest dress, Bess sat next to Rebecca in the hansom cab that was taking them to The Café Royal, where they would meet up with Phineas to celebrate her birthday. As she stared absent-mindedly at the people on the street going about their daily business, a conflicted and confusing mess kept churning in her head.

She thought she should be feeling happy on a day like today. Only she wasn't. The clothes they were wearing and the fine dinner they were going to enjoy – all of it had been paid for by selling another one of Rebecca's silver rings. She had taken it to Mr Sullivan herself.

"*I* should go, darling," Rebecca had said at the time. "It feels wrong to let you do it. That's almost like asking you to pay for your own birthday."

But Bess had insisted. "We agreed that going to the pawnbroker's is my task, and my task alone, Rebecca. Just because it's my birthday doesn't change that."

This arrangement had been Bess' idea originally. She wanted to spare her mistress the shame and humiliation of visiting the pawnbroker's as often as they did. And so she had decided she would be making those trips by herself and without Rebecca. Despite some initial protests, Rebecca had eventually given in, albeit reluctantly.

How long would they be able to keep this up, she wondered – not for the first time. Their lives had begun to resemble one of those melodramas Rebecca used to star in. Except in their case, there was no sign of a noble saviour coming to rescue them. Life was not like the make-believe world of the theatre, she sighed.

She snapped out of her dark broodings when Rebecca laid a gentle hand on her arm. "What's the matter, darling? You're much too young to be looking this serious on your birthday."

"I was just reflecting on some things," Bess said, trying to smile apologetically. "And it seems to have put me in a funny sort of mood."

"Birthdays will do that to you sometimes," Rebecca answered in that warm, caring voice of hers. "And let's face it, this one is rather special for you, isn't it? Twenty – I can hardly believe it."

"I know. Seems like only yesterday I was that smelly little street girl you took home."

"Exactly! And here you are now: a young woman on the verge of adulthood." Rebecca looked at her with eyes that sparkled with pride. "It's high time we started thinking about your future."

"My future?"

Rebecca nodded. "I may not be your mother, darling, but I do feel some responsibility for you. And I realise I have neglected what you might call my maternal duties towards you."

"Your maternal duties?" Bess chuckled. "Now you've got me worried, Rebecca."

"Oh, don't laugh, sweetie," Rebecca said, trying hard to suppress her own smile. "I can't expect you to be my maid for the rest of your life. You'll be an old spinster if you're not careful!"

They giggled like they had often done in the past, back when life seemed easy and carefree.

"Seriously though, darling. Won't you be wanting a husband soon?"

The question took Bess by surprise. "I'm not in any hurry," she answered truthfully. "And besides, I'm–" She felt her cheeks growing hot. "I'm not quite sure I like the idea of giving myself to a man."

Rebecca smiled at her. But those green eyes of hers seemed to be peering straight into Bess' heart. "Do you feel that way because of my special gentlemen friends?"

Bess hesitated briefly, and nodded.

"Not all men are like that, you know," Rebecca said softly. "There are bound to be a few out there who would give you the love and respect you deserve." She gave Bess' hand an encouraging squeeze and the two of them smiled at each other.

Then a mischievous twinkle flickered in Rebecca's eye. "How do you feel about Phineas?"

Bess flushed an even deeper red and turned her face away, her reaction betraying more than any words could have conveyed.

Phineas! She hadn't been able to get him out of her mind ever since laying eyes on him at the station. Everything about him had seemed so perfect to her. His bright smile, his piercing emerald eyes – he was almost a younger, male mirror image of Rebecca.

She cleared her throat and, in an attempt to distract herself and to draw the topic of conversation away from Phineas, she asked, "But what about you, Rebecca? Has there never been a man among your gentlemen friends who you thought might have made a good husband?"

Dreamily gazing ahead of her, Rebecca smiled. "Actually, there is."

Bess' mouth dropped open in surprise, as she grabbed Rebecca by the arm. "Why, you secretive minx," she giggled. "You never told me!"

"What's there to tell?" Rebecca shrugged. "Chief Inspector White is a calm, affectionate and charming gentleman. The mature and civilised type. And he tells me he really loves me."

"He sounds perfect."

"Almost, yes. Unfortunately, he's also married. It's one of those unhappy, strategic marriages of convenience, obviously, arranged long ago by his and her family. But that's all water under the bridge now."

"He could divorce her," Bess suggested. "People do that these days, you know."

"Not when you're a Chief Inspector at the Metropolitan Police, darling. Perhaps if his dear lady wife had the decency to drop dead..." She grinned wryly. "But even then, I wouldn't want Albert to ruin his career by doing something silly like marrying me. Can you imagine the scandal it would cause?"

They fell into a bittersweet silence that lasted until they arrived at the restaurant. Phineas stood waiting outside and he waved at them when they alighted from their cab. Rebecca played the part of the eternally cheerful and dazzlingly glamorous aunt perfectly.

"Happy birthday, Miss Morgan," Phineas greeted Bess warmly, gently pressing her hand.

"Thank you, Mr Parker," she smiled shyly.

"Darlings, listen," Rebecca broke in. "Would you both do me an enormous favour? Please stop calling each other 'Miss Morgan' and 'Mr Parker' like that." She pulled a face mimicking a snooty nobleman. "You sound like you've come straight out of a Jane Austen novel."

Phineas laughed heartily, but all Bess could manage was to blush. Her awkwardness soon melted away however, and their dinner turned into a proper celebration. Rebecca regaled them with stories of her and her sister's upbringing as orphans raised by their grandmother, followed by her life in the theatre. And Phineas told them about growing up with his parents and his two younger sisters. Although his childhood had been nowhere near as dramatic or sensational as his aunt's, Bess found herself drinking in his every word and gesture.

By the time dessert was brought to the table, her head was spinning. And she wasn't sure if it was due to the wine, or because of Phineas and his lovely face.

"Aunt Rebecca," Phineas said, his tone more serious. "I've been wondering."

"About what, dear?"

"I mean no offence or disrespect, naturally, but why did your plays stop being successful?"

"I've asked myself that question many times, darling. Perhaps the audience simply grew tired of me. Or maybe I'm just not a very good actress."

"That's not true, Rebecca," Bess protested. "You're excellent at your craft!"

"That's what I was led to believe as well," Phineas said. "I've been digging up reviews of your earlier plays in the library archives, and the newspapers back then all agreed Rebecca Sutcliffe was a talented star."

When Bess smiled at him gratefully, they held each other's gaze for a brief moment that sent her head spinning even harder.

"That's very sweet of you, darlings," Rebecca replied. "And you're right of course. It wasn't because I went out of fashion or because I'm not good enough. The plain and ugly truth is my later plays were nothing but cheap rubbish, knocked up in a hurry so the organisers could get my name on the poster and sell more tickets."

Bess thought of Walter Huxley. He was partly to blame for that as well. How she loathed the man!

Phineas dabbed at the corners of his mouth with his napkin and cleared his throat. "Aunt Rebecca, perhaps this is utter foolishness of me, but what if I wrote a new play for you? Would you mind awfully if I tried?"

"Mind?! Darling, I'd be honoured!"

"I can't promise it'll be any good though," he cautioned quickly.

"Darling," Rebecca laughed, taking his hand. "It couldn't possibly be any worse than some of the stinkers I have played in."

"Marvellous," Phineas exclaimed. "I've already got a few ideas I'd like to run by you, if I may?" He called over one of the waiters and asked for a pencil and some paper.

Shortly after, he was scribbling and chatting away about potential characters and story lines with so much gusto that anyone watching them would have sworn he was a professional playwright with years of experience.

Bess and Rebecca sat listening to him, enthralled by his energy and his conviction. And when Rebecca threw Bess a quick sideways glance, they smiled at each other.

Chapter Nineteen

"Adieu," Rebecca lamented as she reclined melodramatically on the leather chaise longue. "Adieu, fair world!" She covered her face with a painted fan and collapsed. The small handful of people around her stood frozen, each striking a suitably horrified dramatic pose. And then the stage curtains fell on this final scene.

The audience immediately leapt to their feet, cheering and applauding so loudly the deafening noise seemed to reverberate through the entire theatre building. Ladies and gentlemen alike had tears in their eyes, moved by the heartrending story they had just watched. And everyone sensed that they had witnessed something extraordinary this evening.

Bess stood in the wings with Phineas, watching as Rebecca and the other actors on stage took bow after bow. Standing close beside him in the darkness, she could feel his excitement. She herself was trembling with emotion.

"Oh, Bess," he said ecstatically, as he turned to her and squeezed her arms. "They love it! The audience loved our play!"

An elated '*Yes*' was the only reply she could manage, being too overwhelmed to say anything more.

"We did it, Bess," Phineas raved. "My goodness, we did it. Aunt Rebecca is back!"

Yes, she is, Bess thought as she suddenly burst out in tears of joy and relief. For months, they had been slaving away at turning this new play into a reality.

'The Lady With The Painted Fan' had been their last hope and so they had put their hearts and souls into it. Bess had personally sewn most of the costumes, with the help of Mrs Roberts. And Phineas had been writing and polishing bits of dialogue until the very last rehearsal, just to make sure everything was perfect. Now, all their hard work, worries and anxiety had come to a triumphant close.

"Bess, what's wrong?" he asked, full of concern, when he saw her crying.

"Nothing," she smiled with tear-filled eyes. "Nothing's wrong, Phineas. On the contrary. Everything is wonderful. It's all so fabulous."

Relieved, he laughed and took out his handkerchief, offering it to her. She gratefully accepted it and dabbed at her tears. He could never understand the full depth of her joy, she realised. Having no knowledge of his aunt's secret life as a courtesan for wealthy gentlemen, he didn't know of their anguish or the years of misery she and Rebecca had gone through.

Which is probably for the best, she thought as she smiled at him and gave him back his handkerchief, moist with her happy tears.

After a few rounds of encores and more roaring applause, the cast finally appeared backstage, where people rushed towards them to shower them with praise and congratulations. Rebecca, obviously, got the lion's share of the attention and the compliments. But as soon as she could tear herself away, the actress came over to Bess and Phineas, looking almost delirious with jubilant pride and happiness.

"Darlings," she squeed, opening her arms and pulling them both into a fond embrace. "Isn't it marvellous? Just like old times. Thank you so much."

Before releasing them, she whispered in Bess' ear, "Everything will be just fine again, my lovely. Our troubles are over."

They smiled at each other and Bess nodded, convinced in her heart that Rebecca was speaking the truth.

"This calls for a smashing celebration, darlings," Rebecca said. "We're all going to The Blue Boar for a night of revelling. You'll both join us, won't you?"

"Well, I—"

"Please say that you will, Bess! You and Phineas are the two people I love most in this world, and after a performance like tonight's, I simply must have you with me."

Although she didn't care much for loud parties with lots of people, Bess didn't want to deny Rebecca the pleasure of her company. So she readily agreed to tag along when the entire troupe left the theatre and went to take over the large backroom of the nearby tavern.

To her relief and excitement, this provided her with the added benefit of being around Phineas for a while longer. Sticking close to his side, Bess contented herself with slowly sipping a light cider. Which also gave her the ideal vantage point to observe people while they talked, drank, sang and laughed. Phineas was extremely considerate and stayed with her the whole evening.

"Are you all right?" he asked on several occasions. "If there's anything you need–?"

"I'm perfectly happy, thank you," she answered each time. And she meant it too. Her place was in the background, she knew, as she wouldn't feel comfortable in the limelight.

Phineas kept trying to have a decent conversation with her, but they were constantly interrupted by people who wanted to have a word with the young man who wrote the play that had made Rebecca Sutcliffe a star once again.

Even Walter came over for a chat, his breath reeking of alcohol. "Here he is! The miraculous playwright, they're calling you, my boy." Holding a glass of wine in one hand, he wrapped his other arm around Phineas' shoulders.

"Oh, I don't know about that, Mr Huxley," Phineas grinned modestly.

"But you are," Walter insisted. His speech was slurred and he tripped over his own words a few times. "A veritable miracle worker you are, young Mr Parker. With my vast experience of the theatrical business and your writing talent, why, we'll make a star out of your aunt the likes of which this world has never seen before."

He made a broad sweeping gesture with his free arm, spilling wine over the floor and nearly over Bess' clothes as well.

"Mark my words," Walter prattled on. "We'll perform this play at the grandest theatres all over the nation... and beyond! Far beyond."

Mumbling out loud about his dreams of fame and glory to no one in particular, he toddled off and went back to hover around Rebecca.

"I think Mr Huxley might have had one or two drinks too many," Phineas chuckled.

"I'll say," Bess concurred, eyeing Walter with contempt and mistrust. The producer seemed every inch the desperately jealous suitor, guarding Rebecca against the affections of other men.

Bess despised him for not having tried harder to save Rebecca's career when they needed it. In fact, she couldn't remember him doing much at all. In her opinion, Walter Huxley was weak and spineless; a craven opportunist.

At some point after midnight, Bess told Phineas that she was too tired to carry on. Rebecca however clearly hadn't had her fill yet.

"I don't want this night to end," the actress laughed. "Life is so wonderful right now and everybody loves me. Even the critics were assuring me earlier that they never once doubted my talents – those miserable, lying weasels."

"I'm getting rather fatigued as well," Phineas said. "Shall I escort Bess home, Aunt? I realise it's not entirely appropriate perhaps–"

"Nonsense," Rebecca giggled. "You're family and I trust you to behave like a perfect gentleman with my darling assistant."

"Don't come home too late, please," Bess said, although she didn't blame Rebecca for wanting to enjoy every moment of her rekindled glory.

When Phineas and Bless climbed into the cab he had managed to hail, she had no idea what the hour was. But the streets were mostly deserted and a thick, chilly fog had settled over the city, so they covered their legs with the blanket the driver kindly gave them.

By the time the carriage stopped in front of Mrs Edwards' house, Bess had dozed off. She woke up with a start, discovering to her embarrassment that her head was resting on Phineas' shoulder. Luckily, he had the good grace to pretend he hadn't noticed.

"I'll get out here with you if I may," he said while paying the driver. "The short walk to my lodgings will do me good."

They watched the hansom cab disappear into the dark fog and then smiled somewhat awkwardly at each other. Bess was grateful for the late hour: with Mrs Edwards safely in bed, the meddlesome landlady wouldn't be spying on them from behind her curtains.

"Thank you for taking me home," Bess said, eventually.

"My pleasure. Thank you for the enjoyable evening."

"I'm afraid I didn't contribute much to the proceedings. These busy social affairs really aren't my cup of tea."

"I feel the same," Phineas smiled. "Bess, erm... I–" He cleared his throat and straightened his shoulders. "I would like to see you more often."

"I think we'll see plenty of each other in the weeks and months ahead, don't you? The play seems bound to run for many more nights and I'm sure Rebecca will want you to start writing the next one."

"That's not quite what I meant." Tenderly, he took her hands in his. "Bess Morgan, with your permission, I would like to begin courting you."

"Oh." Her heart started beating faster, while a rosy blossom rose to her cheeks. She swallowed and whispered, "Yes, I would like that too, Phineas. Very much."

His face lit up with that captivating smile that seemed to run in their family. "That's wonderful! You've made me so happy. We'll have to ask Aunt Rebecca to be our chaperone of course. But I'm sure she won't mind."

They giggled and said their goodbyes. After tearing herself away from him, Bess went inside. Her legs were tired and aching, but she floated up the stairs as if her feet had grown wings.

Chapter Twenty

The morning sunshine was already casting its golden rays across the room when Bess woke up. Although she had only been able to get a few hours of rest, it had been a deep and sound sleep with pleasant dreams of a happy future with Phineas and Rebecca. Yawning and stretching, she rolled over and lazily opened her eyes, expecting to find an exhausted Rebecca lying by her side.

But to her surprise, the spot next to her was empty. She sat up with a jolt, suddenly wide awake. "Rebecca?" she called out, looking round the small room. But it was abundantly clear that she was all alone. Rebecca was nowhere to be seen and there was no sign or trace that she had slept in their bed.

Jumping out of bed, Bess washed her face and put on her clothes in a hurry. Perhaps it had been too late to find a cab, she reasoned to herself. In which case Rebecca would have taken a room at the tavern. Bess thought she was fairly sure The Blue Boar had rooms for the night.

One thing was for certain though: it was simply unthinkable that Rebecca had spent the night with someone. She didn't even do that with her special gentlemen friends.

Forcing herself to calm down, Bess started combing her hair. Rebecca was a wise and experienced woman, she told herself; she would be fine. There was no need to worry. "And who knows," Bess chuckled. "Maybe they stayed up all night and the celebration is still going."

Actors were known to do that sort of thing and she wouldn't have put it past Rebecca. Especially not after yesterday's sensational opening night. "Let her have her fun," Bess decided with a smile. "She's earned it."

When she had finished doing her hair, she checked their supplies in the pantry – fully expecting Rebecca to show up later that morning, badly in need of strong black coffee and a hearty breakfast.

"We could probably do with more eggs and freshly baked bread," she spoke out loud, wanting to fill the emptiness of the room with words. "I'd better pop over to the market quickly and buy some."

Taking a shawl and her grocery basket, she went down the stairs while her head was full of sweet thoughts about Phineas. She would have to tell Rebecca what he had asked her on the doorstep the previous night. And she imagined how happy this was guaranteed to make her mistress. Rebecca hadn't exactly been subtle in hinting at the possibility of romance between her nephew and her assistant. The prospect made Bess giggle, just as she reached the bottom of the stairs.

She was halfway to the front door when the door to Mrs Edwards' parlour opened. "Good morning, Miss Morgan," the landlady greeted her, sounding even more stern and rigid than usual.

"Good morning, Mrs E," Bess beamed back cheerfully, determined not to let her happy mood be ruined by this horrible woman.

"My sincere condolences, Miss Morgan."

"I beg your pardon?"

"My sincere condolences," Mrs Edwards repeated. "I was sad to learn of your loss."

"My loss?" This conversation was taking a very confusing turn, Bess thought.

"Do you mean to tell me you don't know yet?"

"Mrs Edwards, I'm afraid I haven't the slightest what you're talking about. I got home rather late yesterday and I'm ashamed to say I've only just risen."

A look of surprise was followed by a wicked grin, before Mrs Edwards quickly straightened her face again. "I see," she said. "It's all over the newspapers this morning, but of course you wouldn't have read them yet."

"Mrs E, please. What's happened?"

"I'm afraid Miss Sutcliffe has been found dead," the landlady announced coldly. "Murdered, apparently. The papers said the police are appealing for any witnesses to report at the station in Broad Street."

Speechless, Bess stared at Mrs Edwards in disbelief – her eyes wide open and her entire body trembling with terror. Leaving the landlady to her own wits, she rushed to the front door and into the street. This couldn't be! It had to be some sort of bad dream she was having, brought on by the late night revelling and all the excitement. Any moment now, she would wake up and find herself lying in bed, drenched in cold sweat, but with Rebecca safe and sound beside her, peacefully asleep.

Unfortunately, she didn't wake up from her nightmare. Not even when she entered the police station on Broad Street and stepped up to the desk of the duty sergeant.

"I was told Miss Rebecca Sutcliffe has been murdered," she said breathlessly.

The sergeant eyed her with the stony expression of a man who has seen too many fools, drunkards and lunatics in his career. "Just about every newspaper in London has reported on the case this morning, yes."

"I'm her assistant. Miss Sutcliffe didn't come home last night."

"That would be on account of her being murdered, Miss–?"

"Morgan. Bess Morgan. I've been living with my mistress for years."

"In that case, Miss Morgan," the police sergeant said drily while getting up from his seat, "I believe the inspector will want to take your statement. And since it sounds like you were familiar with the victim, you'll need to identify the body. That is, if you think you can stomach that sort of thing."

Bess was shown into a more quiet room, where someone offered her a chair and a hot cup of tea. Two men in uniform then entered the room and introduced themselves before sitting down at the table with Bess.

"Morning, Miss Morgan. I'm Inspector Moore and this is Constable Cole. We would like to ask you a few questions if we may."

Bess nodded, wrapping her icy hands around her tea. The inspector asked her all about the previous evening and night, mainly practical things such as the order of events, who was present and what Bess had seen. Sitting next to the inspector, Constable Cole wrote everything down.

Once Bess had told them as much as she could remember – leaving out, of course, the more intimate details of her conversation with Phineas – the inspector shared their side of the story.

"Just before the hour of dawn, Miss Sutcliffe's body was found in an alley quite close to The Blue Boar. Our medical man says she couldn't have been dead for more than a couple of hours."

"Do you know what happened to her?" Bess asked timidly. She hadn't shed a single tear yet, which she presumed was because the shock of Rebecca's death still needed to sink in.

"She was strangled," the inspector replied. Bess faintly registered his words, but they didn't stir any noticeable response in her.

"We haven't got much to go on so far," he continued. "But my guess is someone tried to rob her, she resisted naturally, and then her assailant killed her. Nasty business, but we see it more often than the public realises."

Bess stared at the table, her mind empty. She was vaguely aware of an emotional storm brewing somewhere in the back of her head. But she chose to suppress that for now. The time for tears and sorrow would come later, she had no doubt.

Inspector Moore cleared his throat. "There is one more formality we would respectfully ask you to go through, Miss Morgan."

She looked up at him and waited.

"Miss Sutcliffe was fairly well known obviously, so we are reasonably satisfied it's her. But it would be helpful nonetheless if you could positively identify the body for us. Do you feel up to the task, Miss?"

Bess took a deep breath. "I think so, Inspector."

"Then follow me, please."

The two of them went to the mortuary, where a dead body was laid out, covered with a rough linen sheet. Without taking his eyes off Bess, Inspector Moore carefully lifted the sheet for her, revealing the pale face of Rebecca.

And that's when it hit her full on: the shock she had been waiting for. Bess broke down in tears and buried her face in her hands, shaking and trembling all over; wishing she had never seen the horrible sight that she feared would haunt her in her sleep forever.

"My apologies for putting you through this, Miss Morgan," Inspector Moore said. "So you can confirm that this is indeed the body of Miss Rebecca Sutcliffe?"

"Yes," she answered in between sobbing cries. "It's her. That's Rebecca."

"Thank you, Miss. One more question if I may." He led her away from the covered up body and showed her to a table where Rebecca's belongings had been laid out.

"Miss Sutcliffe had money in her purse and she was wearing several rings. So we aren't sure if the murderer actually managed to steal anything from her. Can I ask you to examine her personal effects to see if any are missing?"

Bess looked them over, recognising Rebecca's rings, a powder case and other small items she usually carried with her. She frowned. Something was missing.

"Her jade necklace," she said. "Where's Rebecca's jade necklace?"

"We didn't find any necklace, jade or other, upon her person I'm afraid."

"But she was wearing it yesterday. I'm sure of it. That necklace was like a good luck charm to her. And she always wore it on opening night." Her jade necklace had been the only piece of jewellery Rebecca insisted they would never sell, no matter how dire their finances became.

"We shall add the information to our case file," the inspector said. "I assume whoever robbed Miss Sutcliffe took that necklace and then fled, frightened off by the viciousness of his own deed. He was probably some young guttersnipe trying to rob his first victim. As I said, it's nasty business, this."

He thanked Bess for her help and promised to keep her informed of any progress in the investigation.

"Although I wouldn't get my hopes up if I were you, Miss. Much to my regret, most of these cases remain unsolved. Unless we find a witness or there's some unexpected development, we will likely never know who killed your mistress."

Moments later, Bess found herself out on the street, dazed and hardly aware of anyone or anything around her. In the space of a few hours, her life and her newfound happiness had been obliterated – wiped out by the hand of a foul murderer.

Chapter Twenty-One

Rebecca's funeral proved to be a greater ordeal for Bess than she had imagined. Having to bear her own grief and sadness over the loss of her dearest friend was hard enough. But she hadn't counted on the huge crowd of onlookers that materialised on the day.

"Who are all these people?" she muttered under her breath at Phineas, who didn't stray from her side.

"Probably perfect strangers for the most part," he shrugged. "I'm assuming they've read about Aunt Rebecca's murder in the newspapers and now they want to see her funeral for themselves."

"But that's unseemly," Bess hissed, trying to hide her anger and disgust. Why did these people have to come here, to the cemetery: a place where the dead were laid to rest for eternity? Didn't they know a burial was supposed to be a sober and respectful affair? She realised Rebecca had been somewhat of a celebrity. But didn't people understand that the nearest and dearest would want to be left in peace on an emotional day like today? Apparently not, by the looks of it, she bristled inwardly.

All these people did was gawk and stare and gossip. She could feel their eyes on her as well, piercing and staring, while they pointed their finger at her and whispered, "There's her maid. Poor girl. So sad, so tragic." As if she were a freakish curiosity at a travelling circus.

Those wretched newspapers were to blame, she thought. Nearly every day, they had been writing about the horrific murder and tragic life of Rebecca Sutcliffe. In their hungry desire to fill their columns and sell more copies, they had gone into great detail about the rise and fall of Rebecca's theatrical career. They had lamented what an immense tragedy it was that such a talented actress should be snatched away from us in one foul, swift act. And just when her fame and glory had regained its former soaring heights. Shameless hypocrites, the whole lot of them!

Seething and fuming silently like this, Bess felt enormously frustrated that all the unwanted attention prevented her from bidding a decent farewell to her most beloved Rebecca: the woman who had changed her life, back when little Bess Morgan had been nothing but a penniless, dirty orphan girl.

She thanked the good Lord above for having Phineas right beside her for support. Several times, she felt so overcome with dizziness and emotions, that she needed to lean on his arm. And when Rebecca's coffin was lowered into the ground, Bess nearly fainted. But luckily, sweet and gentle Phineas was there to steady her.

After the burial, as soon as Bess and Phineas stepped away from the grave, a group of news reporters immediately came swarming over to them, peppering them with questions. Phineas did his best to keep the journalists at bay, politely asking them to consider his and Bess' grief. But still the questions kept coming.

"Miss Morgan," one reporter asked with an arrogant smirk. "Don't you feel this sort of violent end to Miss Sutcliffe's life was to be expected, sooner or later, given her line of work and her colourful lifestyle?"

"What?!" Bess couldn't believe her ears. The brutality! The utter disrespect! A red hot rage exploded inside her as she screamed, "Are you saying, sir, that getting murdered was my mistress' own fault?"

"I don't know, Miss Morgan," the man answered with an impish sneer. "Wasn't it though?"

She let out a furious shriek and flew at him, intent on scratching his eyes out. But Phineas managed to grab her before she could do the man any harm.

"Let me tear that evil tongue out of his nasty mouth," she howled, while bitter tears streamed down her face.

"He's not worth it, Bess. Come, let's go somewhere more peaceful." Gently, he tried to manoeuvre her away from the group of reporters, who seemed greatly amused by this spectacle and Bess' angry outburst.

"Apologies, gentlemen," Phineas said tactfully. "You will have to excuse Miss Morgan. I'm afraid she is overcome with emotion." He gave out a few of his calling cards and said, "Please take my card, in case you would like to speak to me at a later time."

Having had their fun, the reporters let them go as Bess and Phineas moved far away from the crowd.

Standing in a quiet corner of the cemetery, hidden from prying eyes by a small private mausoleum, Bess broke down completely. Phineas pulled her into his arms and she buried her face in his chest, sobbing uncontrollably.

"Why are people so mean?" she asked in tears. "So savage?"

"Who will tell?" Phineas spoke soothingly. "They didn't know my aunt. Not really. They didn't see the person behind the celebrity. They never knew her kindness like you and I did. And they never got to hear her laugh or see her smile in that special way of hers."

His words brought back memories and visions of Rebecca, which helped Bess to calm down.

"Thank you," she said, once she had regained her composure. "You've been most kind to me today. I don't think I could have got through this without you."

He lifted up her chin with his finger and smiled at her. "You know how I feel about you, Bess."

She stared into his soft, emerald eyes. With him, she would always be safe, she thought. Her heart started beating faster and she began to wonder how sweet the taste of his lips on hers would be.

Someone close by cleared his throat and spoke, "Miss Morgan?"

For a minute she feared it would be another news reporter, coming to pester them with more troublesome questions. But when they looked round, they saw a neatly dressed and middle-aged gentleman who smiled apologetically at them.

"I hate to disturb you at this difficult time," he said, politely removing his top hat. "But I wanted to pay my respects to you. Away from all that nonsense back there." With his expensive walking stick he pointed in the general direction of Rebecca's gravesite.

"Thank you, Mr–?"

"White," he introduced himself. "Albert White."

Bess gasped. He was the Chief Inspector Rebecca had mentioned on their way to her birthday celebration a few months earlier. The one gentleman friend for whom Rebecca harboured a genuine love and affection.

"I can tell by the look on your face that you have heard of me," Chief Inspector White smiled.

"Yes, Rebecca spoke about you, sir. And can I just say, Chief Inspector, I am pleased to make your acquaintance."

"The pleasure is entirely mutual, I assure you, Miss Morgan. Rebecca often talked about you whenever she and I happened to discuss our private lives. It was clear that she cared deeply for you."

He fell silent and Bess thought she could see the corners of his eyes beginning to glisten with tears. She gathered that he too had to be struggling with fond memories of Rebecca, the woman he had secretly loved and yearned for.

I have to tell him she loved him too. He should never doubt that. Rebecca wouldn't have wanted it.

"And I know for a fact, sir, that Rebecca was very fond of you. Very fond indeed. I was familiar with her innermost secrets, Mr White, and please believe me when I tell you that she held a special place for you in her heart."

He nodded and stared at the ground in silence, fighting back his tears. After a while, he looked up again and said, "Thank you, Miss Morgan. Her death is a great loss for everyone." He put his hat back on and greeted them with a straight back. "If I can ever be of any assistance to you, please do not hesitate to seek me out."

They watched him leave as he walked, slowly and dignified, towards the cemetery gate.

"I wasn't aware my aunt knew such important people," Phineas said, clearly impressed. "A Police Chief Inspector no less. Seemed like a very nice man indeed."

Bess smiled. Phineas didn't need to know the ugly truth about his aunt's secret life, she decided. Not yet anyway. She would hold that off for as long as she could.

"I wish every policeman was as kind and helpful as him," she sighed. "Because Inspector Moore certainly isn't."

"Still not putting much effort into the case, is he?"

Bess shook her head. Fresh tears threatened to force themselves to the surface, but she pushed them away. "No, he isn't. Says the police are frightfully busy and claims there's nothing more they can do as long as they don't receive any new information."

"I think I saw his face in the crowd at the funeral, incidentally. Say, do you think we should ask Chief Inspector White if he could intervene?"

"Moore would only tell him the same thing. But in a more polite way, obviously."

They sighed and stared at the graves around them, unsure of their next step – until a bold idea came to Bess.

"If Inspector Moore wants new information before he'll consider lifting a finger, then why don't we give it to him? Phineas, we should conduct an investigation of our own!"

"I suppose it wouldn't hurt to ask a few questions here and there. People might be more willing to talk to us than to the police."

"We should start with The Blue Boar," Bess said, her excitement and determination growing. "Because that's the last place you and I saw Rebecca. And her body was found in an alley nearby. Oh Phineas, let's go now! Please?"

"It's been a trying day for both of us, Bess," he cautioned her. "I wouldn't want you to have another breakdown like you had in front of those news reporters back there."

"I won't! I promise."

"I know you want to do this to honour Aunt Rebecca's memory. But let's not do anything rash. We need to have a clear head if we are to find out anything useful."

"But–"

"Right now, your emotions are too raw, Bess. And your pain is too fresh. So I suggest we go for a calming walk in a nice park today. And then we'll visit The Blue Boar tomorrow."

Bess took a deep breath and let it out with a great sigh. "I guess you're right," she said, sulking. But her mood improved quickly, when Phineas offered her his arm and took her to the nearest park.

They walked for a long time, reminiscing about Rebecca. Bess even managed to smile when Phineas pointed out his aunt would have been their chaperone on a pleasant social outing like this.

And even though they both missed Rebecca's presence greatly, somehow they sensed her spirit might have been with them.

Chapter Twenty-Two

The next day, Bess and Phineas went to The Blue Boar, the tavern where they had all celebrated the successful opening night of Rebecca's play. They had strategically timed their visit so the place wouldn't be too busy. The landlord was a friendly man and, just like Phineas had predicted, he proved to be more than happy to talk to them.

No, he hadn't been able to tell the police much. Yes, he remembered their party well. What a merry old bunch they had been. No, he hadn't paid much attention to their comings and goings. He had been working in the main taproom himself that night. But yes, he had caught glimpses of Miss Sutcliffe a few times. A lovely lady, she was. Shocked, he'd been, when he heard about her tragic death the next morning. Simply dreadful what some people were capable of. Hanging wasn't good enough for the likes of those. Drunken brawls among the riffraff of the slums were one thing. But to cut off the life of a cultured lady in cold blood, just for a few pennies? Why, it didn't bear thinking about!

Satisfied that the man's tongue had been loosened, Phineas asked him whether he had seen Miss Sutcliffe leave that night.

Yes, he had, matter of fact. He remembered it well, because the lady had taken the trouble of personally thanking him for the excellent service provided to their party. So kind of her. Such beautiful green eyes as well. And a smile that made you feel like she thought you were the grandest person on earth.

Did he remember if she was alone?

No, she hadn't been on her own. That gentleman had been with her. The one who always had an air of importance about him. Seemed to be glued to Miss Sutcliffe the entire night.

Mr Huxley perhaps? Walter Huxley, the theatrical producer?

Yes, that had been the one. He and Miss Sutcliffe had left the tavern together.

"We must speak to Walter next," Bess said once they were outside again. "We have to know what happened after he and Rebecca left. He's perhaps the last person who saw her alive."

"Apart from her killer, that is," Phineas said as he stared in the direction of the alley where his aunt's dead body had been found.

Walter Huxley lived in a stately, white-faced terraced house that stood in one of the loftier areas of the city – the kind where a constable would shoo you away if you looked even remotely like you had no business of being there.

After Phineas had pulled the bell chord, Bess seized his arm and begged, "Will you do the talking, please? Walter and I don't like each other very much. And I'm afraid I'll speak out of turn."

"Of course," he smiled at her reassuringly, just as one of the servants opened the door.

Walter welcomed them in his opulent sitting room. He rose from his seat when they entered the room, pressing a handkerchief to the corners of his weeping eyes.

"Oh, my poor children," he wailed melodramatically, "I haven't been able to stop crying ever since the funeral. At this rate, I shall deplete my grieving body of its precious fluids within a week and die as a withered corpse. But then at least I would join my beloved Rebecca!"

Bess rolled her eyes at his absurd theatrics, but Phineas remained friendly and courteous. "We all miss her terribly, Mr Huxley," he said sympathetically. "Do you happen to remember around what time she and you left The Blue Boar that night?"

Walter slumped in his seat and draped the back of his hand over his forehead. "The memories are still so painful to me. I can't recollect the precise hour and it could have been anytime between midnight and dawn. But Rebecca left shortly before me."

Hearing the latter, Bess immediately sat up a bit straighter. That's not what the landlord had told them! She opened her mouth to say something, but Phineas spoke sooner – and more tactfully.

"So you don't know whether my aunt managed to hail a cab or if she decided to walk?"

"No, I'm afraid not. Oh, I feel so maddeningly guilty, you know! I should have accompanied her. You must deem me foolish for allowing her to wander the streets alone that late at night? I for one will never be able to forgive myself for this tragic lapse of good judgement on my part."

"You mustn't be too hard on yourself, Mr Huxley," Phineas said.

But Bess couldn't contain herself any longer. Her patience had run out. "That's not what we heard," she snapped angrily. "We spoke to the landlord of The Blue Boar and he told us you and Rebecca left together."

His debilitating grief suddenly forgotten, Walter struck an offended pose. "Then the landlord is wrong, dear Miss Morgan. Rebecca and I left separately. Is that why you've come here? To cast your nonsensical suspicions upon me? Next I suppose you'll be saying I murdered Rebecca."

"Did you?"

She heard a sharp intake of breath from Phineas. "Bess–"

"Miss Morgan! How dare you? I knew Rebecca far longer than you did. And I made a star out of her."

"No, you didn't! Rebecca did all the hard work. You're nothing but a–"

Trying to defuse the situation, Phineas swiftly interrupted her. "You'll have to forgive Bess, Mr Huxley. Rebecca's death has affected her."

"It's affected me as well, I can tell you. But why did you go back to The Blue Boar, my boy?"

"Since the police seem to be at a loss, we've taken it upon ourselves to ask a few questions left and right," Phineas explained. "And when the landlord at The Blue Boar told us he had seen you and Rebecca leave the tavern together, naturally we wanted to talk to you next. To clarify matters."

"And this is clarifying matters, is it?" Walter bristled. "You coming to my home and throwing all sorts of slanderous accusations at my feet? Who are you to discredit my word? I'm a businessman and a theatrical producer with decades worth of experience, but you would sooner believe some tavern keeper instead of me?"

"Mr Huxley, we didn't mean–"

"You should leave the investigating to the police. What a queer thing indeed if a maid and a clerk turned playwright think they are capable of solving a murder case." He laughed arrogantly and looked down at them.

"Quite frankly, Phineas my boy, I must say I'm disappointed in you. I hadn't expected anything different from the girl." He nodded in Bess' direction and turned his nose up at her.

"After all, she was raised in the gutter. But you, a promising young man who had the benefit of a fine education, you should have known better. Shame on you, Phineas!"

He stood up, indicating their visit had come to an end. "Shame on you for going round accusing respectable people, based on nothing more than the hazy memory of some alcohol-loving brute."

Moments later, Bess and Phineas were out on the street again, while the butler threw them a hostile parting glare and closed the door with a bang.

"Well, that went rather smoothly, didn't you think?" Phineas said with a cynical grin. "I may just have destroyed my career as a playwright before it even started."

"I don't trust Walter, Phineas."

"You think he was lying?"

"Who seemed more honest to you: the landlord of The Blue Boar, or Walter Huxley?"

"Mr Huxley's reaction was rather forceful and over the top, wasn't it?"

"Exactly. Why did he claim Rebecca left the tavern before him, when someone else saw them leaving together? He's hiding something."

"It does seem a bit strange," Phineas agreed. "So what do you suggest we do about it?"

"We need to tell the police. Inspector Moore said he wanted eyewitness accounts and new developments? I say we have both."

Unfortunately, Inspector Moore looked decidedly bored and indifferent when they told him of what they had learned.

"So you see, Inspector," Bess said when she and Phineas had finished their story, "you must pay Mr Huxley a visit immediately. Speak to him and press him for all he knows."

The inspector didn't reply straight away. He pursed his lips, tapped his pencil on his desk and stared at them through narrowed eyes.

"It is a dangerous matter, Miss Morgan and Mr Parker –sheer folly even– when members of the public begin to interfere with an official police investigation."

"But Mr Huxley is clearly lying!"

"The differing accounts are nothing but a minor discrepancy. One that can easily be explained by the inaccurate recollection of either of the gentlemen in question."

"Walter is hiding something."

"Such as? Murder perhaps, Miss Morgan? Preposterous! Why would he strangle his own star?"

"I don't know. Why don't you ask him yourself?"

"That wouldn't do, Miss Morgan. No, this is a simple case of robbery resulting in manslaughter.

And I am convinced that we shall apprehend the culprit as soon as he attempts to sell that missing jade necklace. We've alerted all of our informers and as many fences and pawnbrokers as we can."

"Inspector–"

"And in the extremely unlikely event that this was a crime of passion... Well, we all know actresses often choose to frequent certain social circles."

"What is that supposed to mean?"

"I've heard rumours that Miss Sutcliffe was no stranger to this indecent practice. If one of her well-connected gentlemen would happen to have had a hand in her unfortunate death–" He raised his hands and shrugged his shoulders. "Then that would make this case a hornet's nest. And I have neither the desire nor the intention to stick my nose in that sort of thing. Good day!"

"Bess, what was the inspector on about?" Phineas asked. "What did he mean by Aunt Rebecca moving in certain social circles with well-connected men?"

Not for the first time that day, they found themselves standing outside on the pavement again, angry and confused.

Taking a deep breath, Bess decided she couldn't keep hiding the truth from him. He deserved to know. So she told him about Rebecca's secret life as a courtesan and how his aunt had entertained a small and select circle of wealthy gentlemen – to make ends meet and because society seemed to think actresses were that sort of woman anyway.

He listened to her in silence, but he took it well, she thought.

"This... This is obviously quite a shock to me," he said, haltingly at first. "I had no idea."

"Does this change your feelings for her? Do you loathe her now? Many people would, you know."

"No, not at all," he replied firmly. "Aunt Rebecca did what she felt she needed to do in a world that didn't look favourably upon her. It would be wrong of me to judge her that. If anything, I respect her even more. She was a strong woman."

When a wave of relief came washing over Bess and threatened to bring fresh tears to her eyes, he embraced her.

"I was so worried you'd hate her if you knew the truth," Bess whispered.

"Never," he said. "I wish I'd known sooner. When she was still alive. Then maybe I could have done something to help. I wish—"

"It's no use wishing, Phineas. Lord knows I've tried. But no amount of wishing is going to bring her back."

"So what do we do now?"

Bess sighed. "I don't know anymore. But I'll have to find a new position first. I need the money."

"Any idea about what sort of work you'd want?"

"Rebecca always said I'd make a good lady's maid, so that's what I'll look for."

"You'll need a reference letter from your previous employer. Since I'm one of my aunt's closest relatives, I'll write it for you."

"Thank you, Phineas," she smiled. "That's sweet of you."

"Anything to help, Bess."

They gazed into each other's eyes. And for a brief glimmer of a moment, they could almost pretend that all was right in the world.

Chapter Twenty-Three

Sitting across from each other at a small desk in the housekeeper's modest office room, Mrs Johnson smiled at Bess. "I'm quite happy with what I have heard from you so far, Miss Morgan. You sound like a sensible, calm and conscientious young woman. Just the sort of person Mr Davies needs to look after his old mother."

"Thank you, Mrs Johnson," Bess smiled back at her. "That's most kind of you." On the outside, Bess seemed perfectly composed and confident. Inside however, she felt like shaking from anxiety. She kept her hands neatly folded in her lap and she constantly had to remind herself to breathe slowly, to stop her nerves from showing. But she was relieved to hear the interview appeared to be going well.

"I shall read your reference letter now, if I may," the housekeeper said. "And then we can proceed to discuss the duties that will be expected of you."

"Certainly, Mrs Johnson. And thank you."

The housekeeper began to read the reference Phineas had provided for Bess, casually making light conversation while her eyes scanned the letter.

"So sad your previous employer passed away. Did you enjoy working for her?"

"Oh yes, Mrs Johnson. Serving her was a great pleasure."

"Miss Sutcliffe..." The housekeeper frowned and tilted her head slightly as she read Rebecca's name out loud. "Why does that name seem to ring a bell?"

Bess shifted in her seat. "Miss Sutcliffe was the actress who died recently under rather tragic circumstances. You may have read about it in the newspapers?"

The polite smile instantly vanished from the housekeeper's face. "I see," she said, stiffly sliding the reference letter back to Bess over the smooth surface of her desk. "Miss Morgan, this position requires a candidate of the highest moral standards."

Her posture had become rigid, while her tone of voice was icy and distant. Bess didn't understand the sudden change, but deep down she knew her chances had been ruined.

"Mrs Johnson, I can assure you–"

"I am quite convinced, Miss Morgan, that Mr Davies wouldn't want his mother to have a lady's maid who used to be in the service of an *actress*." She virtually spat out the last word – her disgust and disapproval evident in her entire being.

"Even more so," she added primly, "when the actress in question was murdered in a filthy alley behind a tavern like a common trollop."

"Rebecca wasn't a trollop," Bess shot back angrily.

Mrs Johnson rose from her seat and spoke haughtily, "I suggest, Miss Morgan, that perhaps you would be better suited to serve as a maid to some lady-proprietor of a house of ill repute."

"Thank you for the advice, Mrs Johnson," Bess replied as she too stood up. "Perhaps such a lady would have better manners and more grace than you." She picked up her reference letter. "No need to show me out. I still know where the door is."

Seething with rage, Bess decided to walk home rather than take the omnibus. It was cheaper and it gave her a chance to vent her anger by marching at a brisk pace.

Halfway into her journey, outrage had turned into resentment. And by the time Mrs Edwards' house came into view, all that was left in Bess' mind were sadness and despair. She realised she would need to move to cheaper lodgings if she couldn't find a new position soon.

But the thought of leaving behind the place she had called home for twelve years filled her with dread. Because it would also mean leaving behind precious memories about Rebecca and their life together.

Tired and dying for a hot cup of delicious cocoa, Bess entered the house. She prayed that she could avoid running into Mrs Edwards, but the door to the landlady's front room opened almost as soon as Bess came into the hallway.

"Ah, Miss Morgan. I was hoping to see you."

"Good afternoon, Mrs E. The rent is only due next week, isn't it? Or did you kindly want to remind me, so I wouldn't forget?"

Ignoring the barb, Mrs Edwards pretended to be all smiles and said, "That kind gentleman from the theatre, Mr Huxley, was here earlier. He left a parcel for you."

Walter? With a parcel? Perhaps he had wanted to apologise after the argument they'd had last time. Although that seemed highly unlikely. Walter Huxley was more the type of man who preferred to stoke up the fires than to make amends.

Mrs Edwards handed Bess a smallish parcel wrapped in rough packing paper. "He said it contains a few personal belongings of Mrs Sutcliffe's from her dressing room at the theatre. And he generously wanted you to have them, despite –and these were his words, mind, not mine– your appalling abusive behaviour towards him recently."

"Thank you, Mrs E," Bess said absent-mindedly. The contents of the parcel felt soft when she squeezed it gently. *Probably Rebecca's stage clothes,* she thought. But why had Walter bothered to bring them over?

"It won't do, you know," Mrs Edwards said.

"Pardon?" Bess asked. In her mind, she had already dismissed the landlady's presence.

"To be rude and abusive to perfectly nice people like Mr Huxley, Miss Morgan. Tut tut tut. It simply won't do. That's not how you will endear yourself to others."

"I shall endeavour to bear your advice in mind, Mrs E," she replied as she went to the stairs. That hot cup of cocoa would be most welcome when she got to her room.

"By the by," the landlady said. "How did your appointment go?"

Making an effort to be polite, Bess stopped on the stairs to answer. "I'm afraid they have decided to offer the position to someone else." Strictly speaking, that wasn't a complete lie.

"Oh dear," Mrs Edwards grinned. "I hope you'll manage to gain new employment eventually, Miss Morgan. Because as you rightly pointed out, rent *will* be due next week."

"You needn't worry, Mrs E," she said with a curt nod before hurrying up the stairs. In her room, Bess threw off her shawl and hat and placed the parcel on the table. She needed cocoa first!

When her dark and bitter brew was ready, she stirred in two extra spoonfuls of sugar and took her cup over to the table. "Let's see what's in this parcel then," she said after a careful sip.

She undid the string and opened the parcel. Just as she had suspected, it contained the clothes Rebecca had worn on stage. *I remember sewing these,* she thought sadly as she took the dress to admire her own work. But when she held it up, something fell out of the parcel and onto the floor. It had looked like–

She bent down.

And when she laid eyes on the object, she had the shock of her lifetime. There, before her, was Rebecca's jade necklace!

With trembling fingers, she picked it up. It was broken at the lock and she gathered it must have snapped off when Rebecca's attacker tried to take it.

How on earth had it fallen into Walter's hands? Had he found Rebecca's body shortly after the crime? And had he taken the necklace as a gruesome souvenir?

But then why hadn't he called for help? Why hadn't he told the police?

Unless...

Walter was the one who killed Rebecca!

I knew it! I knew he was hiding something.

But why? Why had he murdered Rebecca? The woman he claimed to adore more than anything in life.

And why had he given Bess the necklace? Was this some sort of cruel and twisted trick of his? Was he taunting her?

She was so shocked and so caught up in her frantically racing mind, that she didn't hear the doorbell downstairs, shortly afterwards followed by the sound of voices in the hallway below.

Phineas, she thought as she put the necklace down on the table again. She had to speak to Phineas about this. He would know what to do. And the police had to hear of it as well. Immediately.

Just as she was grabbing her things to dash out, someone knocked on her door. "Miss Morgan," her landlady's voice said. "The police are here to see you. Kindly open this door at once."

When Bess unlocked and opened her door, she found herself face to face with Inspector Moore, who was accompanied by two sturdy looking constables.

"Good afternoon, Miss Morgan. Mind if we come in?" Without waiting for her reply, he stepped into the room.

"Inspector Moore," Bess said, half-relieved yet confused about the purpose and the timing of his visit. "You're just the person I needed to see."

"Am I now?" He nodded at his men, who immediately proceeded to search the room.

"What's the meaning of this?"

Before the inspector had a chance to answer her question, one of the constables called over to him. "Sir?" He was holding up the necklace.

Inspector Moore turned back to Bess. "We received an anonymous tip from a concerned member of the public," he spoke sternly. "And since we have found you so flagrantly in possession of Miss Rebecca Sutcliffe's stolen necklace, we hereby arrest you on suspicion of murder."

"Murder? You don't understand," Bess gasped as the constables seized her by the arms. "Walter put that in the parcel," she shouted, struggling fiercely. "Tell them, Mrs E! Tell them Walter left it here for me today."

Inspector Moore looked at Mrs Edwards, who stood in the doorway wringing her hands. "I only know Mr Huxley delivered a parcel," she replied. "And very kind about it, he was too. But I really couldn't say if that stolen necklace was in it. I couldn't say even if you asked me swear to it in a court of law."

Bess was furious. "This is all Walter's doing," she screamed. "He did it! He murdered Rebecca. And now he's trying to blame me."

With crazed and burning eyes, she looked at Inspector Moore and hissed, "I bet he's the one who sent you that anonymous tip."

The inspector merely sighed and shook his head. "I wouldn't know, Miss Morgan. But why don't you come with us to the police station? Quietly. And then you can tell us all about how you obtained Miss Sutcliffe's necklace."

With a look of mock horror and barely concealed glee, Mrs Edwards watched Bess being taken away.

"And to think I provided board and shelter to a murderer! Tut tut tut. Maids strangling their mistresses for their valuables. What is this world coming to?"

Chapter Twenty-Four

The courtroom was packed with spectators, whispering excitedly about the trial that was about to start. All tickets had been sold out in a matter of hours and people were jostling for the best viewing spots, intent on getting the most out of the proceedings. The members of the jury sat squeezed tightly together, and even Bess felt hemmed in with two constables surrounding her and almost pressing up against her.

Her hands were shackled, which only added to her deep sense of misery. Luckily though, she could see Phineas from where she was sitting. *Thank heavens for his kind face,* she thought, trying to steel herself. His was the only friendly face in a sea of onlookers who already seemed convinced that she was the murderer.

Phineas had offered to pay for a defence lawyer, but Bess had refused. She knew he would have gone into debt for her and she didn't want that. Justice would be served, she told herself. The truth was plain to see after all. They didn't need an expensive lawyer to demonstrate that.

The whispering and chattering intensified when the judge entered the room. He called for order, and then the trial began. The first witness was the medical doctor who had examined Rebecca's dead body. He testified calmly about the marks found on the throat of the victim and stated that the cause of death had been strangulation, estimating the murder to have occurred no more than a few hours before dawn.

"In your medical opinion, Doctor," the judge asked, "based on those marks on the victim's throat, can you tell whether the murderer was a man or a woman?"

"I cannot rule on that with complete certainty, My Lord. However, I will say that the marks appeared consistent with an individual possessed of moderate-sized to somewhat smaller hands."

"So it could have been a woman?"

"That is a possibility, My Lord, yes."

The eyes of the judge and the jury all turned to Bess, sending a chill up her spine. *They've already made up their minds,* she gasped silently.

"Or a man with smaller hands," she added fervently. *A man like Walter Huxley,* she wanted to shout.

"That too is a possibility," the doctor admitted, sounding somewhat uncomfortable with the cold gaze of the judge on him.

One of the jury members rose to his feet and asked, "Doctor, could a young woman possess the strength to strangle her victim?"

"It would depend on the physique of both the murderer and the victim of course. But in this case we have strong reasons to believe the victim had been consuming generous amounts of alcohol that night. And this would undoubtedly have made any attempts at resistance from her part considerably less effective."

"Splendid," the judge smiled. "So we have it from a medical expert's mouth that the murderer could well have been a woman. Thank you, Doctor. Our next witness is Police Inspector Moore."

The inspector reported on his investigation into the murder, including how the police had discovered the stolen jade necklace in Miss Morgan's room.

"Quite a damning piece of incriminating evidence, wouldn't you say, Inspector?" the judge asked.

"Indeed, My Lord. Although Miss Morgan strenuously denied having taken the necklace, naturally."

"Naturally. A murderer rarely admits to her crime instantly, doesn't she?"

"That is my experience as well, My Lord."

"Did the accused have any explanation as to how she came into the possession of the victim's necklace?"

"She did, My Lord."

"And what was her story, Inspector?"

"She claimed Mr Huxley gave it to her, My Lord."

"This would be Mr Walter Huxley, the theatrical producer with whom the victim enjoyed a long-standing professional collaboration?"

"The very same, My Lord. Miss Morgan claimed Mr Huxley had delivered a parcel containing the stolen necklace at her address shortly before we paid her a visit."

"How convenient," the judge remarked.

"And this wasn't the first occasion on which she attempted to implicate Mr Huxley, My Lord. Previously, she had used a vague discrepancy between witness accounts to accuse Mr Huxley of 'hiding something', as she put it."

"He *was* hiding something," Bess shouted. "He said–"

"Silence, Miss Morgan! In my court you will behave yourself. And you will control your feminine tempers."

Eyeing her sternly, the judge smoothed down his dark robes and turned back to Inspector Moore. "Inspector, on those occasions you've just mentioned, did the accused imply or claim in any way that Mr Huxley murdered Miss Sutcliffe?"

"She did, My Lord."

"Rather a baseless claim, wouldn't you say?"

"Yes, My Lord. Why would Mr Huxley murder his own star? It doesn't make sense. That's like killing the goose who laid the golden egg."

"Tell us, Inspector, when were your suspicions about Miss Morgan first roused?"

"Oh, straight from the beginning, My Lord. During her initial questioning, the morning after Miss Sutcliffe's murder, Miss Morgan's behaviour seemed cool and emotionless. Not at all what one would expect from a supposedly devoted maid who has just found out her mistress has died."

"Especially a maid who has proven herself perfectly capable of strong emotions," the judge added, casting an accusing glance at Bess.

"Precisely, My Lord. Take, for instance, Miss Morgan's striking conduct at the funeral, where she appeared to be scowling the whole time. At one point, she even went so far as to attack innocent members of the press."

"Thank you, Inspector." The judge turned to address the jury, made up entirely of well-dressed middle-class men. "In conclusion, gentlemen, I believe Inspector Moore has painted a clear and convincing picture of the accused as a shrewd, cool and calculated individual."

"That's not fair," Bess yelled.

"Furthermore," he continued, ignoring her angry outburst, "the accused has demonstrated, abundantly, that she has very little control over her passions. This Court now calls Mr Walter Huxley as a witness."

Ever the showman, Walter had to be supported by two people holding his arms when he strode over to the witness stand. Haltingly and seemingly overcome with emotions, he told his story. He spoke of his relationship with Rebecca, both as her producer and most staunch supporter, as well as her dearest friend and confidant.

Bess interrupted this farce several times, angrily calling him a liar and a hypocrite. But each time, the judge silenced her.

"I should warn you that my patience with you is running thin, Miss Morgan," he snapped eventually. "If you wish to ask the witness a question, you may do so – respectfully! Otherwise, I strongly suggest you hold your tongue."

He turned back to Walter. "We appreciate this must be hard for you, Mr Huxley. But please do not let yourself be intimidated by the accused's uncouth behaviour. I shall not stand for that sort of thing in my court."

"Thank you, My Lord," Walter said with a trembling voice. "I remember feeling equally upset during Miss Morgan's visit to my home. She caused such a violent commotion, I was terrified it would give my poor elderly mother a fatal fright. My staff will gladly testify to this if required."

"I am certain that won't be necessary, Mr Huxley. We'll take your word for it. You were telling us about the affection and admiration you held for Miss Sutcliffe?"

"Indeed, My Lord. For nearly two decades, I was absolutely devoted to Miss Sutcliffe. And I am not ashamed to admit my feelings extended on a personal level as well." He paused and sighed. "Alas, Miss Morgan has always been envious of that deep and special relationship. She wanted Rebecca all to herself."

"Have you any proof to substantiate that statement, Mr Huxley?" the judge asked, sounding like a caring parent patiently talking to a child.

"Miss Sutcliffe confessed as much to me, My Lord."

"Please explain."

"I had long ago made clear my desire to marry her, although she always bid me to wait. Recently however –that is, before she was tragically murdered–"

Walter had to stop in order to dry his tears and blow his nose. Then he took a deep breath and continued, "Recently however, as she became wiser and more mature, Miss Sutcliffe had expressed an inclination to accept my marriage proposal."

Bess let out an irritated snort to express her disbelief, which immediately earned her another scowling glare from the judge.

"But," Walter sighed, "she said she was afraid of how her jealous maid, Miss Morgan, would react."

"Liar!"

"Miss Morgan," the judge bellowed, banging the table with his fist. "That was the last outburst to come out of your crass mouth. Not another word from you, or so help me God, I shall have you flogged."

Several of the jury members were shaking their heads as they looked at her in what was clearly a sad and disapproving manner.

"Born in the slums," Bess overheard one of them saying to the man next to him. "What else can you expect?"

His neighbour nodded. "Barely human, these people."

Chapter Twenty-Five

Wringing her hands and looking pleased to be at the centre of attention in the crowded courtroom, Mrs Edwards tried her hardest to present herself as the humble little matron courageously doing her bit in the fight against crime.

"Now then, Mrs Edwards," the judge said. "I understand you used to rent a shared room to the late Miss Sutcliffe and the accused."

"That is correct, My Lord. I was their landlady for many years. And had I known that one of them would turn into a cold-blooded murderer, I would have turned them out of my house immediately. I run a respectable establishment."

"I'm sure you do, Mrs Edwards. You say you've known the accused for a long time?"

"Ever since she came to live with Miss Sutcliffe, My Lord. That must have been some twelve years ago. Poor Miss Sutcliffe! Out of the decency of her noble heart, that sweet woman took mercy on a dirty street urchin. And how does the wicked child repay that kindness? By murdering her mistress! Awful, I say."

"We haven't quite established the accused's guilt yet, Mrs Edwards," the judge said calmly. Then he smirked and added, "We'll get to that part soon enough though."

Bess heard several members of the audience and the jury chuckle. She wanted to scream about the unfairness of it all, but she bit her tongue.

"Mrs Edwards, as a longtime acquaintance of Miss Morgan, will you please give this Court your honest impression of the accused's character?"

"Certainly, My Lord."

"However, before you do so," the judge said, holding up his hand to stop her while he turned to Bess, "Miss Morgan? I'm hereby giving the constable permission to hit you over the head if you utter so much as one foul or angry word. Do you understand?"

"Yes, My Lord," she replied resentfully and much to the amusement of her former landlady. Satisfied, the judge nodded at Mrs Edwards to continue.

"Even though it goes against my nature to speak ill of people, My Lord, I must admit there is precious little good I can say about Miss Morgan. She was extremely vain and always showing off every new dress Miss Sutcliffe generously gave her."

Bess grumbled, but when she sensed the policeman by her side readying himself, she decided to remain quiet.

"You mention Miss Sutcliffe's generosity, Mrs Edwards," the judge said. "Did you have the impression she was a woman of means?"

"She did her best to pass as one, My Lord. There's no doubt about that. Although the pair of them often did seem to have monetary difficulties. They never failed to pay their rent, mind you – I have a very strict rule about such things – but I believe they were quite well known at the local pawnbroker's."

"We will hear from Mr Sullivan shortly, have no fear. Before you go, Mrs Edwards, can you tell us whether you noticed anything unusual about the accused around the time of Miss Sutcliffe's murder?"

"As a matter of fact, I did, My Lord."

"Pray tell."

"On the morning after Miss Sutcliffe's most tragic death, Miss Morgan's demeanour was remarkably happy."

"Happy, you say?"

Mrs Edwards nodded vigorously. "Not a care in the world, My Lord. Struck me as exceedingly odd, it did."

"You may step down, Mrs Edwards. You have been most helpful, thank you. The Court calls Mr Sullivan, owner of Sullivan & Son Pawnbrokers."

Mr Sullivan was a kind and unassuming man, who now seemed frightfully uncomfortable with so many eager eyes upon him as he took to the witness stand. Bess felt sorry for him. The pawnbroker had always treated her and Rebecca with respect. Perhaps his testimony would help to shift the balance back in her favour?

"Mr Sullivan, it is this Court's understanding that the late Miss Sutcliffe and her maid were regular customers of yours. Is that correct?"

"It is indeed, My Lord. I had the honour of receiving them in my shop on a regular basis."

"How regular, Mr Sullivan?"

"In later years, up to three times per month, My Lord."

"That often, eh? And what sort of items did you buy from them?"

"Mostly jewellery, My Lord. Various different types of pieces. Rings, pearls, necklaces, brooches, pins, bracelets – that sort of thing. Always of the highest quality, I should add."

"Valuable stuff?"

"Absolutely, My Lord. Professional discretion forbids me to state the actual sums involved, but they were often quite substantial. Especially for the larger pieces."

"Did you never wonder where or how Miss Sutcliffe and Miss Morgan obtained those expensive pieces, Mr Sullivan?"

"At Sullivan & Son we respect our clientele's privacy, My Lord. We do not pry into their personal lives or finances."

"Nevertheless..."

"But nor are we in the habit of purchasing stolen goods. I wish to be very clear on that. Sullivan & Son are not fences and we do not deal with thieves."

"So how *did* Miss Sutcliffe and Miss Morgan obtain those pieces?" the judge insisted.

"I believe they were gifts, My Lord. Miss Sutcliffe had, erm, friends who admired her work."

"I too have friends who admire my work, Mr Sullivan. But they are not in the habit of bestowing expensive jewellery upon me."

"With respect, My Lord, but that might be because you are not a charming, graceful lady."

A ripple of laughter went through the courtroom until the judge gruffly demanded *'Order!'*

"Tell me, Mr Sullivan, did the accused always accompany Miss Sutcliffe on these visits to your fine establishment?"

"She did, My Lord. And in more recent years, Miss Morgan would bring in the pieces by herself."

"Without her mistress? Did this development not arouse any suspicions in you?"

"I saw no need to be suspicious, My Lord. Miss Sutcliffe was a customer in good standing and with a long history of transactions with us. I merely assumed that Miss Morgan, in her capacity as Miss Sutcliffe's assistant, wanted to unburden her mistress with the task of pawning her jewellery."

"What was your impression of the accused during these visits?"

"Miss Morgan was always polite and correct, My Lord."

Bess straightened her slumping shoulders a bit, pleased to finally hear some kind words being said about herself in this trial.

"She did not strike you as nervous? Or agitated? Skittish perhaps?"

"Most people are rather embarrassed to find themselves in a position where they are forced to pawn their valuables, My Lord. Miss Morgan was no different."

"Are you saying, Mr Sullivan, it never occurred to you that Miss Morgan might have stolen those pieces from her mistress? You never thought she was keeping the money to herself?"

The pawnbroker blinked a few times, clearly taken aback by this idea. "N–no, My Lord. That possibility never entered my mind."

"How delightfully naive," the judge chuckled. "I thought a pawnbroker would be a bit wiser to the ways of the world. Surely, you have heard about maids stealing from their mistresses and then pawning the goods?"

"I am not unfamiliar with the phenomenon, My Lord. But I felt I had no reason to believe–"

"Never you mind, Mr Sullivan," the judge said, waving his hand dismissively. "Foolishness is a vice, not a crime."

The pawnbroker blushed, and Bess felt both ashamed and angry at how the judge was treating him.

"One last question, Mr Sullivan. Even though you –unwisely– never questioned the accused's honesty, would you say she was aware of the monetary value of Miss Sutcliffe's jewellery?"

"Oh, undoubtedly, My Lord. Due to the quantity of pieces Miss Sutcliffe and Miss Morgan sold to us over the years, they both had a good grasp of the numbers, so to speak."

"Miss Morgan as well, you say?"

"Absolutely, My Lord. Perhaps even more so than Miss Sutcliffe, as she seemed to possess a more practical mind compared to Miss Sutcliffe's artistic leanings."

"Practical?" the judge asked, looking at Bess. "Or cunning?" He smirked and dismissed Mr Sullivan. It was time to call the final witness.

"Mr Phineas Parker, please!"

Chapter Twenty-Six

Bess could feel her anxious pulse pumping through her veins as Phineas took to the witness stand. He was her only hope now. Her last chance at salvation. She sent up a quick prayer, took a deep breath and looked at Phineas, smiling nervously. Catching her eye, he returned her smile with ease and confidence, as if to tell her everything would be right in the end.

My life is in your hands, sweet Phineas, she thought, trusting him with all her heart.

"You are Phineas Parker, are you not?" the judge asked, "The nephew of the late Miss Sutcliffe?"

"I am, My Lord. Miss Sutcliffe is– *was* my mother's only sister."

"My notes tell me you lived with your father and mother in Essex until fairly recently. What brought you to London, Mr Parker?"

"My father arranged a position as a clerk for me, My Lord. But my ambition is to establish myself as a playwright eventually."

"Theatre must run in your family's blood then. I understand you wrote the play Miss Sutcliffe last performed in? 'The Lady With The Painted Fan' it was called, I believe?"

"Correct on both counts, My Lord."

"Quite successful, I was told?"

"The audience on opening night appeared elated," Phineas replied proudly. "And the reviews were unanimous in their praise for both my aunt and the play."

"Nasty rotten luck, eh," the judge commiserated. "Your aunt getting murdered just when your play was such a success? Must have made you rather cross at the murderer, I presume?"

"I was mostly shocked and sad about losing my beloved aunt, My Lord. The future of my play was the least of my concerns."

Phineas briefly glanced at Bess and then announced to the whole room, "And as for whoever killed Aunt Rebecca, I hope they will get their just deserts."

"That's exactly what we're here for today, Mr Parker," the judge grinned. "Now, I want you to cast your mind back to the night your aunt was murdered. You stated to the police that you were with the accused?"

"That's right, My Lord. Bess– Miss Morgan was by my side the entire evening and I escorted her back to her home late at night. So you see, My Lord, she couldn't have done it. Bess couldn't possibly have killed my aunt, because she was with me the whole time."

His voice had a passionate and pleading tone that Bess found very touching. But it didn't seem to impress the judge much.

"The jury will decide on that matter if you don't mind, Mr Parker," he said. "Can you remember when exactly you escorted Miss Morgan home?"

"Not the exact time, I'm afraid. But it couldn't have been much later than a few hours after midnight. My aunt and a small group of people had decided they wanted to continue their celebration at The Blue Boar."

"So perhaps it was between two and three o'clock at night?"

"That would seem very likely, My Lord."

"And I take it you proceeded to your own lodgings after you had safely delivered Miss Morgan onto her doorstep? You did not –please forgive my rudeness– accompany her to her room?"

Phineas looked taken aback at the suggestion of any impropriety between him and Bess. "Most certainly not, My Lord. I went straight home. And my landlady can testify to that, since I had foolishly forgotten my key and was therefore obliged to wake her up."

"Splendid, Mr Parker," the judge beamed. "Splendid!"

Phineas frowned. "My Lord?"

"I quite like you, Mr Parker. And I would hate to think that you were lying to this Court. But it all fits perfectly, don't you see?"

"I'm afraid I don't, My Lord."

"Miss Sutcliffe was murdered before dawn. Since you escorted the accused home not too long after midnight, this gave Miss Morgan plenty of opportunity to return to the tavern, wait for the victim to leave and then commit her vicious act."

"That's outrageous," Bess shouted, immediately receiving a blow over the head from one of the constables.

"Bess wouldn't hurt a fly," Phineas replied hotly. "Let alone kill anyone. And least of all Aunt Rebecca. Bess loved my aunt more than she cared for herself."

"What about you, Mr Parker? Does Miss Morgan care for you? Speak truthfully now."

Phineas blushed and stared at his feet. "I– I would like to think so, My Lord."

"Of course she does, Mr Parker! My eyes do not deceive me. Don't think I haven't seen the glances you and the accused have been exchanging even in this very Court of Law."

"It's true, My Lord," Phineas said as he stood with a proud, straight back. "I had asked Miss Morgan's permission to begin courting her. I did so that very night in fact. Before any of us knew about my aunt's death of course."

"Evidently, Mr Parker," the judge grinned. "However, I trust you –as well as the gentlemen of the jury– understand how this sentimental attachment to the accused disqualifies you as a neutral judge of her character?"

"She didn't do it! Bess didn't murder my aunt. I know she didn't. I can feel it in my heart," Phineas pleaded with his hand over his chest.

"Love-struck hearts are easily deceived, Mr Parker. You may stand down, thank you."

"But we–"

"Thank you, Mr Parker," the judge repeated sternly.

"My Lord, I insist–"

"Mr Parker!" the judge snapped. "Do you wish to challenge my authority in this Court?"

"No, My Lord," Phineas muttered, lowering his head.

"It's one thing for an infatuated young man to stand up for his sweetheart," the judge bellowed, turning red and sending angry flecks of spittle into the air. "But I shall not tolerate disrespect and disobedience. Not from you or anyone else!"

Meekly, Phineas apologised to the Court and returned to his seat, casting a sorry look at Bess.

You tried, she wanted to tell him.

"We will now hear from the accused, Miss Bess Morgan," the judge called out. "But I must warn you, Miss Morgan," he said, wagging a finger at her. "No temper, no filth and no nastiness!"

Bess cleared her throat and tried to keep her legs from wobbling as she began to tell her tale. She shared the story of her unlucky start in life, when her parents and siblings died and she ended up living on the street with her poorly grandmother – who then also passed away, freezing to death in her sleep.

She spoke of how thrilled and grateful she had been when Rebecca saved her and took her in as a maid and assistant. Careful to avoid the topic of Rebecca's special friendships, she nevertheless told the Court about the good times as well as the bad times.

"And throughout it all, I always remained loyal to my mistress. Leaving her wasn't an option that I would ever have wanted to consider – not for a moment!"

She looked at the blank faces of the jury staring back at her, and threw in every bit of passion that was left in her.

"Miss Sutcliffe saved my eternal soul when she took me off the streets. I could never have betrayed the love and kindness she showed me. I would have done anything for her. Absolutely anything! Had I been present in that alley on the night she faced her murderer, I would have given my life for her – in an instant and without any hesitation."

Picturing the scene of Rebecca's death, all alone in the dark with her killer's hands around her throat, Bess broke down. Pleading her own innocence, pleading for her life after having to endure an unfair trial full of lies – these things had all taken their toll. She cried and could speak no more.

"A very touching story, Miss Morgan," the judge yawned ostensibly. Then he addressed the jury. "Gentlemen, you have all the facts. The doctor has stated the victim could well have been strangled by a woman. Police Inspector Moore has testified to the evil behaviour of the accused."

He held up his hand and began to count the arguments on his fingers. "Thirdly, you have Mr Huxley's statement that the victim was reluctant to accept his marriage proposal... out of *mortal fear* for the accused's reaction."

He raised his voice and stared hard at Bess when he spoke that latter part. But she was too weak, too spent, to say anything and merely cried instead.

"Furthermore, you heard from the accused's former landlady how the savage street urchin grew up to become a vain and immoral young woman. While a respectable business owner has spoken of the accused's sharp and cunning mind. And finally–" The judge paused briefly, enjoying the attention of the entire audience.

"The accused's very own lover had no other choice but to admit that Miss Morgan had the opportunity to murder her mistress."

After another dramatic pause, he went on. "And as for her motive? One unpleasant glance into the accused's black heart would reveal the jealousy and rage that live there. Rebecca Sutcliffe wanted to marry Walter Huxley, but Miss Morgan had no desire to relinquish her pivotal and privileged position in the luxurious life of her glamorous mistress. And so she murdered her."

After looking at each member of the jury individually, the judge concluded, "Gentlemen, the time has come for you to pass a verdict. Guilty or not guilty – that's what I want to hear."

He gave a short wave in the direction of the door. "You may go and deliberate out in the hallway. But don't take too long, please. We have two more murders to get through today."

The jury got up to leave, but they soon found the room to be too crowded for them to reach the door to the hallway comfortably. So they decided to remain seated, huddled closer together and simply conferred among each other in whispered tones.

After only a few minutes, one of them rose and said, "My Lord, we have reached a verdict."

Chapter Twenty-Seven

"Splendid," the judge grinned. "I like it when my juries just get on with it. And how do you find the accused: guilty or not guilty?"

"Guilty, My Lord."

Bess let out a long wail of agony and despair. All was lost! How had she ever dared to hope for any other outcome, when the cards had been so blatantly stacked against her?

"Miss Morgan," the judge spoke, throwing the full weight of his authority into his voice. "You have been found guilty of the murder of Miss Rebecca Sutcliffe, your former mistress. I hereby condemn you to be hanged by the neck until dead."

"Nooooo!" The high-pitched sound left her throat like a prolonged and horrified shriek. She was vaguely aware of Phineas' voice, somewhere in the distance it seemed, shouting angrily.

"Hold your tongue, Mr Parker," the judge barked. "Or I shall fine you for disrespecting this Court. And for heaven's sake, Miss Morgan, stop your incessant blubbering, woman! It's unseemly. Have some dignity."

But Bess didn't care about dignity or any other of his fancy words. Her legs couldn't support her weight anymore and she would have crashed to the floor if the constables by her side hadn't caught her just in time.

"Miss Morgan, you shall be taken from this place and return to your prison cell, where you shall await your execution."

The judge looked round the room and stated solemnly, "Let this sentence be an example to anyone who might be harbouring bitterness or ill will towards their betters in their hearts and minds. And now clear the court so we can move on to the next murder."

Surrounded on all sides by the bustling chaos of people and their animated chattering, the two constables escorted Bess away while the crowd began to leave the room.

"Bess!"

Phineas came pushing through the heaving mass to get closer to her. She called out his name, but one of the constables blocked his passage.

"You'll get a chance to visit your sweetheart in prison before her execution next week, lad," the policeman grumbled. "Now let us pass or I'll give you a taste of my truncheon."

Once they had cleared the busy crowds, Bess was led to the back of the building, where a sinister prisoners' carriage stood waiting for her outside. With its heavy door and tiny barred windows, it didn't look much like a carriage and more like a large black wooden box on wheels.

Or a coffin, she thought darkly.

"Lovely day, innit," one of the constables merrily declared to his colleague while they led Bess down a short flight of stairs.

"It sure is," the other replied, smiling up at the blue sky. "Reminds me of the sort of sunshine we used to get in summertime back when I was a lad."

"We just don't get summers like those anymore, do we?"

The first constable stopped to open the heavy door of the carriage. As the door swung open and revealed the confined space inside, Bess sucked in her breath – fearful like a helpless lamb being taken to the abattoir.

Seeing her terror, the constable laughed, "Your carriage awaits, my lady."

"It's a shame, innit," the other one said with a smirk.

"What is?" his colleague asked, smiling. They were clearly intent on enjoying a bit of cruel banter at Bess' expense.

"That we don't have public executions anymore, I mean. A nice hanging on a sunny day like today? Bound to draw a huge crowd."

They snorted while they kept Bess waiting, her hands still shackled while she stood in front of the open door with the gaping darkness of the carriage beyond it. Despite their mockery, only one conscious thought went round and round in her head. *Next week, I'll be dead.*

The constables were still laughing. "A man could probably make a small fortune selling food and drinks to a hungry crowd like that."

Bess was breathing rapidly and she could feel her heart pounding like mad. *I'm going to die.*

But then a strange, eerily placid feeling came over her, as all other sounds seemed to fade away into the distance and her vision became narrow yet crystal clear.

I mustn't die. I can't die.

"Come on, love. We haven't got all day." Laughing, one of the constables gave her a little nudge in the back to make her get into the prisoners' carriage.

And that's when she felt a surge of raw energy welling up from deep inside of her – like a primaeval power that took control of her mind and her body, screaming at her to live!

She kicked the shin of the constable on her left as hard as she could. And while he cursed loudly and grabbed his painful leg, she swung her shackled fists into the other one's belly, knocking the wind out of him.

Using the momentary distraction, Bess made her escape and legged it out of the back alley. When she emerged onto the busy main street, she could already hear the constables swearing and yelling behind her. And when the first shrill police whistle sounded, she flung herself into the traffic on the street. As a woman condemned to die, she might as well meet her death while trying to escape it, her frantic mind urged her.

She saw quick flashes of cart wheels and frightened horses, while her ears faintly registered the harsh sounds of angry drivers, panicked animals and pursuing policemen. But she made it to the other side of the street unharmed and had even managed to put a little more distance between herself and the handful of constables chasing her. With no idea where to go, she simply kept running.

The police would eventually catch up with her, she feared. Unless she could find a place to hide from them.

Driven by her instincts and a primitive urge to survive, her feet carried her into the slums – never far away in the old heart of the city. This was her true home, no matter how long she had lived in ease and comfort with Rebecca. This was her world. But would it be able to swallow her up and save her?

Haggard looking people with dead eyes, dull faces and dirty clothes gazed at her as if she were an evil phantom. Descending deeper into the rundown neighbourhood, she ran through several narrow streets, always aware of the police on her heels.

"Please, help me," she begged a few times when she saw people hanging around at the front doors of their ramshackle houses. "I'm innocent."

But they just shook their sad heads while their restless eyes spoke of more fear than she was feeling herself. "Don't want any trouble, Miss," they would reply invariably. And so she pressed on, determined to continue her desperate escape until the bitter end.

After she had rounded yet another hopeless corner, someone ran up beside her. "Through there," he grunted, shoving her into a dingy courtyard that didn't appear to lead anywhere. She was trapped!

Gritting her teeth and bent on fighting her way out, she turned on her new assailant. But then she saw the shock of ginger hair, looked at his face and recognised him.

"Joe!"

"Princess," he grinned.

She could hear hurried footsteps echoing over the cobblestones. It wouldn't take the police long to have a look in this courtyard. And then they would catch her.

"Joe, I need your help."

"I can see that," he said, eyeing the shackles around her wrists. "We often seem to run into each other when you're in trouble, don't we? Must mean we're made for each other or something."

"Joe, please."

"Don't worry, love. Joe Thompson and his gang will rescue you."

He whistled and immediately two teenage boys sprung forward from inside a dark recess.

"The lady is coming home with us, lads," Joe told them. "But we need to lose those peelers first. So we're taking a roundabout route. Bill, you lead the way. Tom, you mind the rear."

Without saying a word, the eldest of the two boys went ahead and dove into a doorway. Bess and the others followed. They hurried through a hallway and up several flights of stairs, eventually bringing them to a landing with an open window, where they prudently stepped onto a flat rooftop. After a good few yards, they jumped onto a lower roof and used that to climb into another tenement.

"People will see us if we just go traipsing through their homes like this," Bess whispered.

"And what if they do?" Joe shrugged.

"They'll tell the police!"

"No, they won't. Have you forgotten folks around here don't like the police? Most of them are too afraid to help, but they won't go ratting on you to the coppers."

Down another flight of stairs and they came into a different courtyard, where a colourful variety of washing was hung out to dry on lines that zigzagged across the yard. Joe grabbed a damp shawl from one of the lines as they walked passed and flung it at Bess.

"Wrap this over you and try to cover up those irons on your wrists for now," he said. "I know a good locksmith who can get those off in a jiffy."

"Won't he know the police are looking for me?"

"He won't care. He and I often do business together, if you know what I mean. And I pay him good money not to mind that sort of minor detail."

With the help of Joe's silent companions, they navigated through a maze of alleys, courtyards and winding streets. Bess lost all sense of direction, but after playing cat and mouse with the police for several hours, it seemed their small band had won.

Joe ordered Bill and Tom to double back discreetly and make sure no one was on their trail anymore. When the two boys returned and gave the all-clear, Bess finally dared to let out a cautious sigh of relief.

"We can go home now," Joe smiled.

Chapter Twenty-Eight

Home turned out to be a squalid room on the ground floor of an old, decrepit tenement with walls that were so crooked, it made you wonder why the building hadn't collapsed yet. Bess saw some straw mattresses lying on the floor in one corner, a cooking stove and a table with a few chairs. The only other furniture consisted of a cupboard and a chest of drawers, both of which seemed on the verge of falling apart.

"Welcome to our humble abode," Joe quipped.

A scrawny young boy stood on an upturned crate by the stove, stirring in a bubbling pot with a large wooden spoon. His eyes widened in surprise when he saw Bess. "Who's she?"

Bill and Tom threw themselves down on top of the mattresses and started whispering and sniggering like teenage boys did.

"Georgie, this is Bess," Joe answered. "She's going to stay with us for a while."

Was she? Bess hadn't had time yet to think about what would come next. But she was on the run for the police now. And if they found her, they would take her back to prison – where the gallows were waiting for her.

"Can you cook?" Georgie asked her.

"A bit," she said, giving him a faint smile. His face was covered in a layer of dirt and soot, but his eyes were friendly. She estimated he was about five or six, but children had to grow up and be wise quickly in the slums.

"Will you help me prepare supper then? I'm a rubbish cook myself. Bill and Tom are always complaining about my cooking."

"I'll try," she said. "But I'm not sure how much use I'll be with these things on." She held up her shackled hands for him to see.

"That's all right," little Georgie shrugged as if, to him, escaped convicts wearing iron restraints were perfectly normal dinner guests.

Rapidly warming to this youngest member of the small gang, Bess went over to the stove, while Joe watched and smiled approvingly.

"So what are we making?" she asked.

"Just stew," Georgie said. "Same as always. It's cheap and it's easy."

She sniffed at the aromas rising up from the pot and wrinkled her nose.

"See?" Georgie sulked. "You don't like my cooking either."

"No, it's not that," she lied quickly. "It's just not finished yet, that's all. It needs some more work. That's what cooking is about."

She looked around and asked, "Where do you keep your herbs and spices?"

"What are they?"

"Herbs and spices are things we can add to our food so it tastes nicer and a little more interesting."

Georgie stood and stared at her with his great big eyes, ready to learn everything she would teach him. Looking into those eyes, Bess realised the little rascal had already stolen her heart.

"Why don't you bring out everything you normally use to make supper," she smiled. "And then we'll see what we've got."

"Yes, Miss," he replied excitedly as he jumped down from his crate and rushed to do as he was told, eager to please her.

Working together, Bess did the best she could with the crude and limited means at their disposal. But the others approved of the result.

"Best supper in years," Tom said as he licked his bowl clean.

"Yeah," Bill agreed. "If he keeps this up, maybe our Georgie will grow up to become a cook for a family of toffs in one of them big houses someday," he chuckled.

"I got a lot of help from Miss Bess," Georgie shrugged and blushed.

"I'm glad you liked Georgie's cooking," Bess said. "Now why don't you two boys help him to clear the table and wash up the dishes?"

"That's a woman's job," Bill protested.

Bess grinned and held up her shackled hands. "I'd make a terrible mess and probably end up breaking everything with these, I'm afraid."

"You really need to take her to Charlie, Joe," Bill grumbled. "So he can work on those irons."

"We'll go and see him tomorrow, don't you worry," Joe replied. "But how about you lads do as Miss Bess asks for now, eh?"

"Come on, Tom," Bill mumbled reluctantly. "Seems we're on skivvy duty tonight."

Bess suppressed the urge to laugh, while the boys cleared the table and then went outside to wash up at the nearest water pump.

"They're good lads," Joe said.

"Are they your gang then?"

He nodded. "It's not much, but it's a start. And at least I'm my own man now."

She smiled at how proud he seemed. They were petty thieves, burglars and pickpockets – but they had saved her. Saved her from certain death.

"I haven't thanked you properly yet," she spoke softly. "If it hadn't been for you–"

"Don't mention it," he said with a short wave of the hand. "That's what friends are for, eh?"

Friends, she thought. Was that what they were now?

"Joe, I need to get away from London, I think. Move somewhere else; a big city where no one knows me."

He shook his head. "Bad idea. This murder has received a lot of attention, even before you escaped. And some artist is sure to have sketched you during the trial. So your name and your face will be all over the newspapers in the morning. Wherever you go, people will recognise you."

"But then what do I do?" A heavy sense of hopelessness and despair began to weigh her down again.

"You need to keep quiet for a while. Stay out of sight somewhere safe. Until people lose interest and forget about you."

"And the police?"

"They too will forget about you. Eventually. In a year or two, your case will have dropped so far down their list of things to do, your name won't even cross their minds anymore."

She fell silent. One or two years seemed like an awful long time to her. And what would happen after that? She would still need to leave London and start a new life elsewhere. But she didn't have any money. So how was she supposed to survive in the meantime?

As if he could read her thoughts from the worried expression on her face, Joe cleared his throat. "I've been thinking..."

She looked up at him, her mind blank except for the fear and doubts she was experiencing.

"You'd be safe here," he said. "You could live with me and the lads. People round here don't ask questions. They've got their own troubles to worry about."

He leaned forward and looked her in the eyes. "I'll give you food and shelter and all the rest of it, for as long as you need."

"In exchange for what?" she asked apprehensively.

"Your services."

"My—" A deep red blush of shame and anger sprung to her face. She still remembered the kiss he had extracted from her years ago.

"It's not what you think," he immediately defended himself. "The papers said you were a lady's maid. That means you could cook and clean for us. Wash and mend our clothes. You know, that sort of thing."

"You want me to be your maid?"

"More or less." He got up and stared out of the window with its broken panes. "These lads... They need something I can't give them."

"You mean a mother? Joe, I can't do that!"

"Of course you can. I've seen how good you were with little Georgie. And you seemed to manage Bill and Tom just fine too."

"Joe–"

Listen," he sighed. "I'm not very good with fancy words, so I'm just going to tell you straight." He sat down again, resting his hands and forearms on the table.

"Me and the boys, we're just simple thieves. But I don't intend to die in this filthy slum like every other poor sod. I want us to become gentlemen. Proper like. With manners and such. The sort of stuff *you* can teach us."

"Me?!"

"Yes, you. You're not some ordinary maid, Bess. You used to serve a proper lady. And you're educated. So I want you to teach us to read and write, show us the right clothes to wear, how to speak and how to behave ourselves."

"I don't know if I can do all that, Joe. You're asking a lot."

"All I'm asking is that you give it a try. You don't need to say yes straight away. Sleep on it overnight and let me know in the morning."

When the boys returned, Joe had them drag one of the straw mattresses to the other corner, so Bess would have a small space to herself. But after they had all gone to bed a little while later, she couldn't sleep. Her mind was a whirlwind of worries and doubts and way too many questions.

As it turned out however, she wasn't the only one who was still awake. Amidst the snoring noises of the others, someone stirred. Holding her breath, she listened as a pair of feet padded over to her in the darkness.

"Miss Bess?"

"Georgie?" she whispered.

"I can't sleep."

"What's the matter, darling?"

"I'm afraid I'll have bad dreams again."

"Do you have those often?"

"Yes. And they're always about bad men chasing me and trying to kill me."

"Oh, you poor sweetheart. Tell you what, you can sleep with me tonight. Would you like that?"

Even with only the faint moonlight shining through the window, she could see the little boy nodding his head eagerly.

"Come on then," she smiled.

Georgie didn't need to be told twice and, as far as her shackles allowed, they snuggled up to each other underneath the blanket. *Just like Rebecca and I used to do,* she mused.

"Miss?" he suddenly asked after they had lain in comfortable silence for a bit. "Is it true you killed someone?"

She frowned. "No, I didn't kill anyone, little darling. Why do you ask?"

"We heard people talking by the water pump. They was telling about this woman who had murdered her mistress, but then she ran away from prison. Figured it might be you. What with those shackles and all."

"It's a long story, sweetheart. If I promise to tell you in the morning, will you be a good boy and go to sleep now?"

"Of course, Miss. I'll do anything for you."

"You're very sweet. Good night, Georgie."

"Good night, Miss." He was already dozing off when he added, "I like you."

I like you too, darling.

Perhaps spending some time with Joe and the boys wouldn't be such a bad idea after all. Not for too long of course. Just enough to repay Joe for his help, and for her to come up with a plan.

Her last thoughts before she drifted off were of Phineas. Would he be searching for her?

Chapter Twenty-Nine

"That was an exquisite breakfast, dearest," Joe quipped. Pretending to be a dandy, he dabbed delicately at the corners of his mouth with his napkin. But then Tom belched loudly with his mouth wide open, making the other two boys snort with mischievous delight.

"Thomas," Joe bristled while trying hard not to laugh too. "Where are your manners, lad?"

"Clowns, the lot of you," Bess said as she shook her head and cleared Joe's empty plate. Even though the small gang had come a long way since she had joined their unusual household, they were still undeniably a playful bunch of fools.

Likeable fools, she secretly had to admit. Especially the boys.

"Now see what you've done," Joe said to Tom. "You've upset Miss Morgan." He had become very good at playing the role of the father figure. Even though most of the time, that's all it was: benign posturing and play-acting. Still, Bess thought he was getting rather good at it.

"Sorry, Joe. I'm sorry, Miss Morgan."

"That's better," Joe nodded. "Finish your breakfasts, lads. And then we're off to work." 'Work' as he called it, obviously meant stalking the streets in search of wealthy pockets to pick. "Georgie, it's your turn to stay home with Miss Morgan."

"With pleasure, sir," the little boy replied. "May I be excused?"

Bess smiled at him and nodded, "Yes, you may."

Bill silently mimicked his youngest friend's polite manners, which immediately prompted Joe to raise a warning finger at him. Georgie seemed oblivious to the lighthearted mockery and started helping Bess with clearing the table.

The others got up from their seats as well and put on their coats. "How do we look?" Joe asked Bess.

"Quite dapper," she said as she went over to them for a final inspection.

"My neckerchief is too tight," Tom grumbled.

"It's called a cravat, sweetheart. And stop fidgeting with it or you'll ruin the knot," she admonished him lightly while she readjusted it for him.

Watching them, Bill sniggered.

"And as for you, Bill," Bess said without taking her eyes off Tom's cravat, "have you combed your hair properly or would you like me to do it for you?"

"My hair's fine, Miss," he blushed. "Why do we need to dress like toffs anyway?"

"Because," Joe replied, "as I must have told you a thousand times already, young master William, when we act and look more like toffs, the real toffs won't suspect who we are."

"Yeah, it's certainly made it easier to pick their pockets," Tom chuckled.

"There," Bess declared. "All done."

"Right-o, let's be off then," Joe said. With a wink, he asked, "Georgie, my lad, you'll look after Miss Morgan for us, won't you?"

"You may depend on me, sir!"

"Good man. What's for supper this evening?"

"Miss Morgan and I are making lamb stew, sir."

"Sounds delicious. Well, toodle-pip," he said cheerfully as he put on his hat and opened the backdoor for Bill and Tom.

Bess watched them leave, staring after them through the clean window. *A happy little family,* she thought wryly. *Almost.*

She sighed and turned round, inspecting the room. It too had come a long way. Gone were the dirt and the gloom. It was still the same sparsely decorated affair, but they had a bit more furniture now and she had managed to bring a distinctly homely feel to the place.

She smiled as she saw Georgie sitting at the table, bent over his copybook and looking very serious as he slowly copied a line of words several times. Sensing her gaze on him, he looked up and his entire face lit up like sunshine breaking through the clouds.

"Will you check my work for any mistakes when I'm done, Bess?" he asked eagerly. When it was just the two of them, he usually dispensed with the more formal and polite 'Miss Morgan' and simply called her Bess. She didn't mind.

"Of course, my darling," she said as she came over and glanced over his shoulder. "But I can already see you're doing very well. Your handwriting is so neat and tidy."

He beamed with pride at her and then went back to his work. Bess returned to the stove, where she was heating up a kettle so she could start doing the dishes. She hated the feel of tepid water and that's why she preferred to add some scorching hot water from the kettle to the large enamel washing-up bowl.

While she waited for the kettle to boil, her eyes drifted off toward the window again. She supposed she should be feeling grateful. Because here she was, alive and well, and living in a modest degree of safety and comfort, while she was still on the run for the Law – condemned to death even.

And yet...

Exactly one year after that horrible night when Rebecca died, she seemed doomed to spend her days mostly within the confines of these four walls, staring out of the window – while Rebecca's murderer probably went through life without a care or worry in the world.

It wasn't fair. But she didn't think she had the energy to be angry about it. All she felt was sadness – sadness for everything she had lost: Rebecca, her freedom... and Phineas.

Turning away from the window, she took a deep breath and let it out in a long and audible sigh.

"What's wrong, Bess?" Georgie asked with cautious concern in his voice.

"It's nothing, sweetheart," she lied with an awkward smile. And then, when a sudden idea came to her, she added, "I've just remembered we'll need rosemary for the stew. Would you mind going to the market for me?"

She felt awful lying to someone as sweet and innocent as Georgie, but it was the only excuse she could think of. The room felt like it was trying to suffocate her – even more than usual on a day like today. She needed to get out; to escape this place for a little while. Or else she was sure she would go mad. So as soon as Georgie went on his errand for her, she would dash out to visit Rebecca's grave. Whatever the risks to her.

"I'll do it straight away, Bess," the boy said. "So I can choose the freshest and best possible rosemary for you."

"You're the sweetest, Georgie," she smiled outwardly, while despising herself deeply for her ruse. Watching from her window again, she took the kettle off the stove and waited until the boy had disappeared from view. Then she grabbed her shawl and hurried outside as well – feeling excited, fearful and ashamed all at the same time.

Would the police be on the lookout for her, she wondered while her jittery legs carried her in the direction of the cemetery? Or had they begun to forget about her, just like Joe had predicted they would?

When she spotted a constable standing on a corner, her legs almost gave way beneath her. But to him, she was merely another face in the crowd and he barely looked at her. Nevertheless, she let out a deep sigh of relief when she reached the cemetery without any further fears or incidents.

She quickly found her way to Rebecca's grave and paused in front of it, gazing at the name on the tombstone while her mind opened up a treasure trove of memories; some happy, some sad.

A solitary tear began to roll down the side of her face, as Bess whispered, "I miss you, Rebecca. Oh dear Lord, how I miss you."

"Bess?" a soft voice behind her spoke affectionately.

She would have let out a frightened cry, if she hadn't recognised that voice.

Phineas!

She spun round, and when she saw his beautiful face, more tears came flowing. He looked at her, clearly struggling with a mess of conflicting emotions: puzzled, delighted, and simultaneously sad.

"I was hoping I would find you here today," he said, his tone warm and caring. He glanced briefly at the tombstone. "Hard to believe it's been a year, isn't it?"

Unable to face him, she nodded and turned her eyes away, wanting to hide her tears from him.

"I'm relieved to see you again, Bess. I've been so worried. And then when the police couldn't find you, after a while I became anxious that something bad might have happened to you."

She shook her head and tried to smile. "No, I got help."

"Thank heavens for that. Who helped you?"

"An old friend. But please don't ask me more. It's best if you don't know. That way, if the police ever question you about me, you won't need to lie."

That was true enough, but it was also a good excuse to not have to divulge anything about her arrangement with Joe. She had no idea how Phineas would react if he heard about that one.

"I understand," he said. "I'm just happy to hear you escaped safely and to see that you're alive. You look well, incidentally."

"That's kind of you to say, Phineas," she grinned. "It's an outright lie, but kind anyway." The difference in appearance between them was like night and day, she thought. Where she looked pale and haggard, dressed in drab clothes that made her seem like a colourless skivvy, he was every inch the up-and-coming young gentleman. She felt ashamed to even stand close to him.

"You, however," she continued, admiring him. "You look very dashing if you don't mind my saying so."

"Thank you. I've already managed to sell a few plays and they seem to have done rather well."

"That's great to hear, Phineas. I'm very happy for you."

"Mr Huxley wanted to produce one with me as well. But I refused. It wouldn't feel right to take money from–"

He paused.

From the man who murdered your aunt? Bess completed his sentence silently. *No, I wouldn't think that would feel right at all.*

She decided to push any thoughts about Walter aside and smiled, "With your success, I bet droves of swooning mothers are lining up their eligible daughters for you."

A rosy colour shot up from his neck to his cheeks. "No, there's only space for one in my heart." He paused and avoided her eyes.

Too ashamed to tell me he has moved on and found himself a fiancée, no doubt, she thought, rather sadly.

"Congratulations," she said, trying to hide her disappointment.

He looked up and frowned. "What? I don't understand."

"On your engagement, I meant. Congratulations."

"Oh, no, no. I'm not engaged to be married." He cleared his throat and gently took her hands in his. "I meant there's only space for you in my heart, Bess."

Now it was her turn to blush. But as she quickly looked away from him, out of the corner of her eye, a swift movement in the distance caught her attention.

She had spotted the familiar shape of a young boy hurriedly diving behind a tombstone not too far away from where they stood.

"Georgie," she sighed.

Phineas let go of her hands and tried to look in the direction she had been facing, but he didn't see anyone. "Pardon?"

"My shadow," she said. "He's one of the boys under my friend's care and he must have followed me here."

Phineas' emerald eyes darted round the cemetery, searching for any other potential dangers lurking in the shadows. "Are you sure your so-called friend can be trusted?"

"Please don't worry, Phineas," she tried to reassure him. "Joe would do anything to keep me safe." She had blurted out Joe's name before realising it, and instantly regretted it.

Phineas hesitated. "That's good to hear, I suppose. So this friend, he– He looks after you? Does he take good care of you?"

"Yes, he's been good to me. A gentleman in every way, you might say." She felt awkward discussing Joe with him and she wanted to brush over the topic as quickly as possible. *Let's get back to that place in your heart,* she pleaded to him mentally.

"I'm–" Phineas swallowed. "I'm glad to learn you are safe, Bess." His tone was oddly formal. "And I wish you and Joe well."

She shook her head with vigour. "No, Phineas. It's not what you think. Not at all. He gives me food and shelter, and in return I cook and clean for him and the boys."

"But you... live with him? Under the same roof, I mean. With this... man?"

"Merely as his maid, Phineas." Panic crept into her head and into her voice. She didn't want to lose him all over again.

"But then how–"

They were interrupted when they noticed other nearby visitors were beginning to look their way. A cemetery was not a suitable place to have a quarrel, those inquisitive and disapproving looks said. Especially for young couples without a chaperone.

"I must go," Bess said, the fear of being recognised growing by the minute.

"Wait. When can I speak to you again?"

"I don't know," she answered, tearing herself away from him. "Perhaps it's best if you forgot all about me, Phineas."

"Bess, I can't. I love you."

She stopped and looked at him, torn between fleeing back to safety... and throwing herself into those strong yet tender arms of his.

But, in the end, her panic about the sheer recklessness of her situation won out over the desire in her heart. Crying, she turned around and ran away.

Chapter Thirty

By the time she got home, they were all waiting for her. Joe was pacing up and down the room, clearly seething with anger. The two older boys sat on their mattresses playing cards, while Georgie had contented himself with watching their game. When Bess entered, the little boy looked decidedly miserable and guilty as he anxiously cast down his eyes.

"How could you be so stupid?" Joe asked her furiously.

"It's the first anniversary of Rebecca's death," she replied calmly. She wasn't going to apologise to him for her decision. "I simply had to go and visit her grave."

"Didn't it cross your mind that the police might have had the same idea? They could have been lying in wait for you."

"Only they weren't, were they?"

"No, but what if they had been? They would have dragged you back to prison and hung you by the neck!"

"At least it would have meant the end of my worries."

"Don't say that," Joe snapped. His face was red and she could see thick angry veins standing out in his neck and on the side of his forehead. "And who was that man you were talking to?"

Ah, so he wasn't just angry; he was jealous too!

"No one," she lied. "An old friend."

"Who was he? Tell me his name," Joe demanded. "He might go to the police. He might even have followed you here. For all we know, he could be telling the peelers where you live, as we speak."

She dropped the tone of her voice and said, with a cold and deliberate air of defiance, "Why don't you send one of your little spies to find out?"

"Joe made me do it, Bess," Georgie blurted out with hot tears streaming down his face.

"I know, my darling," she spoke soothingly. "And please don't think I'm blaming you." She turned back to Joe and continued icily, "I blame Joe for being too cowardly to do his dirty work himself."

"Dirty work? Why, the nerve of you! Here I am, trying to keep you alive, but then you go and risk it all by venturing out in public in broad daylight.

And what for? Some foolish sentimental... sentiment."

Seeing him struggle with his words like that, suddenly she didn't want to argue with him anymore. Calmly, she said, "I don't want to be a prisoner and a fugitive for the rest of my life, Joe."

He wasn't willing to give up the fight just yet however. "If the police catch you, your life will be over very quickly indeed. Because you'd be dangling at the end of a rope before the week is over. Is that what you want?"

In his trembling voice, she detected an urgency and a desperateness that triggered something in her. She wasn't afraid; she wasn't even angry at him. Instead, she took pity, while inside her she could feel a quiet and determined power awakening.

"I only want this mad injustice to end," she said. "But tell me, what is it *you* want, Joe? Can you answer that one and truly be honest about it?"

"I don't know what you mean," he grumbled, avoiding her gaze and betraying himself.

"Oh, I think you do know, Joe Thompson. You're just too afraid to admit it to yourself."

"Go on then," he challenged her. "Spit it out, if you're so smart."

"You want us to be a happy little family, Joe." There was no hint of anger or sarcasm in her voice. She knew she was speaking the truth. "You want to be the good king who rules over a glamorous court of princely thieves. But I could never be your queen."

"That's ridiculous."

"Is it, Joe? Because I believe that you were hoping I would fall in love with you, eventually, if you just made me play the part of your wife for long enough."

"My wife?" He turned red again, but this time it wasn't rage that coloured his cheeks. His words came haltingly. "I never– I didn't– I've always treated you with respect and I never laid a finger on you, Bess!"

"I know that, Joe. And I have no doubt that your intentions are honourable." Her voice sounded kind and warm. He had lost the argument, but she would show him mercy. There was nothing to be gained by being mean to him.

"And please believe me when I say I'm eternally grateful to you for saving me from the gallows, and for all the help you've given me. But, Joe–"

He had turned his head slightly sideways, to avoid her intense gaze, but she touched his sleeve so he would look her in the eye for what she was about to say.

"I'll never be able to give you what you really want. This so-called family we have here between the five of us, it's only make-believe. It's nothing but a fantasy."

He tried to turn away again, but she didn't let him. He needed to hear this, no matter how painful the truth was to him.

"I truly and deeply care about you and the boys, Joe. And I want you all to be happy. But there can never be real love between you and I. Not in the way you were dreaming of."

She let go of his arm. He looked devastated and she felt sad for him. "I'm sorry," she said with a wistful smile.

Leaving him alone with his sorrow and his thoughts, Bess went outside. She didn't know what to do or where to go next. In an aggravating and maddening way, the future seemed both wide open and yet impenetrably closed off to her. She leaned with her back to the wall in the courtyard and looked up at the sky. Maybe a good cry would help, she thought. But her body didn't have any tears to shed at that moment. She merely felt empty.

Empty, clueless and hopelessly lost.

The faint sound of timidly shuffling feet brought her attention back down to earth. Georgie looked at her with sad and gloomy eyes. She beckoned him over and pulled him into her arms so they were facing the same way and his back was pressing softly against her belly.

"I'm sorry for ratting on you, Bess," the young boy said with a drooping lip.

"It's all right, Georgie. I understand. Really, I do."

"No, but you see, Joe said he was worried you might do something silly today. And then something bad would happen to you. So he told me that, if you sent me out of the house with some excuse, I was to come back and follow you."

He paused and then said, "It didn't feel right, you know; sneaking behind you like that. But I was worried sick about you when Joe told me. And if the police had tried to arrest you, I would have fought them, Bess."

She smiled. "I know you would have, you brave little hero of mine."

"Are you angry with me, Bess?"

"Of course I'm not angry with you, my darling. You did it because Joe asked you to and because you wanted to protect me."

And you did it very well, she thought, secretly admiring him for his stealth and the way he had managed to stalk her all the way to the cemetery without her spotting him.

After a brief silence, Georgie suddenly asked, "Was she very pretty? Miss Sutcliffe, I mean? I heard she was an actress, so she must have been beautiful."

"Yes, she most certainly was. But not only on the outside. She was beautiful on the inside too."

"Like you?"

"No, much more beautiful than me. I'm nobody. Plain old Bess. Nothing special."

"That's not true," he replied immediately and with conviction. "No one's ever been nicer to me than you have. For me, you're the most beautiful girl in the whole wide world!"

"And you're very sweet," she said, placing a kiss on the top of his head.

"So will you be leaving us soon then? I'll be terribly sad when you do."

"I don't know yet, my love. There isn't really anywhere else for me to go."

Nowhere to call home. No place where she belonged and would feel safe. She thought she'd had a home once. But then that life had been snatched away from her when Rebecca died –

murdered by a man who had succeeded in putting the blame on Bess.

She sighed, pushed off from the wall and let go of Georgie. "I need to go for a little walk," she said. "To clear my mind. If Joe asks, tell him I'll be outside The Grand Theatre."

Thirty-One

Staring at the theatre from the safety of the shadows, Bess thought it looked even more neglected and derelict than it had all those years ago when she first met Rebecca. Or maybe, because her memories of that time had been such happy ones, her mind simply had made the place seem more magnificent than it really was.

Her eyes sought out the door and all the windows and secret entryways she had used as a little orphan girl from the slums to sneak into the building. She smiled as she remembered that girl climbing up to the rafters, where she had the best spot to listen to the actors rehearsing on stage.

And when random pieces of overheard dialogue suddenly came back to her, in Rebecca's enchanting voice, the memory made her shudder.

Sweet Rebecca, she sighed. *What would* you *do if you were in my shoes?*

For one thing, her former mistress wouldn't be hiding in the shadows, Bess thought. That much was for certain. Rebecca would have taken the fight to the enemy, storming into the arena on the back of a chariot drawn by fiery horses with flaring nostrils – like some warrior queen from one of her plays.

The fantastical vision made Bess laugh out loud. Yes, a thing like that would have been *just* like Rebecca. Her friends wouldn't have expected anything less from her.

And it would probably have worked too!

The murderer would have trembled with mortal fear, dropped to his knees and begged for mercy and forgiveness.

A pity she, plain old Bess Morgan, would never be able to do such a thing. She lacked the strength of character, as well as the spirit, to pull it off. Didn't she?

But then again...

Neither could she imagine herself cowering in fear for the rest of her life; hiding from the police in Joe's lair. No, the time had come for her to move elsewhere. Another city perhaps? Maybe in a different country. She could move to Paris or Italy and find herself a wealthy elderly lady to serve.

Or why not even further afield? She had heard stories about people completely reinventing their lives in India or Australia. Over there, no one would ask her awkward questions. When you moved halfway across the world, your previous life ceased to matter.

She supposed she could start by taking on sewing work to earn a bit of money for a boat ticket. And once she got there, she would be able to find a decent position. She was smart enough, she had the experience and, above all, she had the will to do it!

Somehow though...

It didn't seem quite fair to her that she needed to abandon her life and her small handful of friends, just because some pompous, self-important little man had blamed her for the vile murder he had committed.

Why was she the one running away? She was innocent! *He* should be the one living in fear. Walter Huxley was the villain in this mad tragedy, not her.

Squeezing her hands into fists so tight it made her fingers and knuckles turn white, she didn't hear the footsteps coming up behind her.

"Bess?" a voice asked.

Startled, she let out a frightened little yelp and spun around.

"It's only me," Joe said, sheepishly. "Didn't mean to scare you, sorry. I would have thought you'd hear me coming."

Resting her hand on her thumping chest, she let out a sigh of relief. "I was lost in thought."

"Must've been some very deep thoughts then. Mind sharing what they were about?"

"What to do next. What to do with my life."

Joe nodded and said nothing for a while. To give him time to find the words he was clearly searching for, she stared back at the theatre.

"I've been thinking too," he said. "The things you told me at home, they were true. I was secretly hoping you'd begin to love me after a while... The way I loved you."

"Joe–"

He held up his hand to interrupt her. "I realise, now, how that was pretty foolish of me. You can't force love to grow in someone else's heart."

"No, you can't," she replied softly. "But for what it's worth, I respect you for the way you tried. You waited, you were kind and you never did anything... untoward."

"I seem to remember," he grinned, "that I once told you I was a gentleman."

"That you most certainly are," she smiled. "The gentleman-thief."

"At your service, princess," he jested. Then he looked at her more seriously again and said, "I love you, Bess. I know there's no chance you will ever love me back, and I suppose I'll have to get over that. But everything I did, I did it only because I wanted to see you happy."

He took a deep breath and smiled at her. "And I still want you to be happy, Bess. So I've decided I'll help you get your freedom back. Whatever you choose to do or wherever you may want to go."

She took his hands and gave them a fond squeeze. "Thank you, Joe. You're a true friend. And I will always love you, as a friend."

He seemed pleased with that idea.

"So these deep thoughts you were having earlier," he continued. "Anything useful in them?"

She told him about the different directions her wandering mind had been taking her. And how she had reached the conclusion that she wasn't going to run away. She would fight instead.

"I like the sound of that," he replied. "How?"

"That's the problem; I don't know yet."

"Do you think this friend of yours –the one you saw at the cemetery– do you think he might be able to help?"

"Phineas? Possibly. He's clever and he's got a closer connection to Walter."

"Can we trust him?"

"Rebecca was his aunt and he adored her. He's got as much reason to hate Walter as I have."

"Very well," Joe said. "Let's meet up with this Phineas of yours. Three minds are smarter than one."

A cautious sparkle of hope reignited in her heart. "Oh, Joe! Do you mean that?"

He nodded. "Sure do. I'll get one of the boys to deliver a note to him. The sooner we can arrange a meeting, the better. Walter Huxley's days as a free man are numbered."

* * *

They met two days later. After Phineas had been sworn to absolute secrecy, Bill led him from a prearranged street corner to their rented room on the ground floor.

The first few moments were awkward and tense. Although she was overjoyed to see Phineas again so soon, Bess tried hard not to show it, out of consideration for Joe's feelings. But that didn't stop the two young men from regarding each other with suspicion and wariness.

When the introductions and greetings – strained and stiff– were over, the three of them sat down at the table, while the boys vanished outside. Bess decided to speak first, since Joe and Phineas still seemed busy eyeing each other up.

"As our note told you, Phineas, I've decided to fight back. I don't want to hide from the police any longer. We need to bring Walter to justice."

"Excellent. Any ideas yet?"

"Not really," she replied. "It's why Joe felt it would be good for all of us to get together."

"The best solution is always a simple one," Joe stated. "So I say we lure this Huxley to a quiet location where we beat a confession out of him." He banged his fist on the table to put some force behind his argument.

"I'm not sure how I feel about that, Joe," Bess frowned. "It's so... violent and bloody."

"And the police are unlikely to accept a confession like that," Phineas added. "Walter could claim he acted under duress. And that would effectively render his confession null and void."

"All right then, Mr Fancy-Pants," Joe growled. "Have you got any ideas of your own that are more sophisticated?"

"Joe, please," Bess spoke calmingly. "I'm sure Phineas was only trying to help."

"Well, it didn't sound very helpful to me. But if, supposedly, he's this creative genius, then perhaps our friend the playwright can come up with something more inspired?"

"To be honest, I didn't have any ideas at all when I arrived here," Phineas said.

Letting out a short self-righteous 'ha' noise, Joe crossed his arms and leant back in his chair.

"But when you mentioned playwriting," Phineas nodded at him, "I suddenly thought that there might be something in that."

"What do you mean?" she asked.

"Don't tell me you're going to write a play about it," Joe scoffed, earning him a reproachful stare from Bess.

Phineas gazed into the distance, his mind clearly working hard on an idea that was taking shape.

"Not quite," he replied vaguely. "But it will involve some theatrics and a bit of drama."

Bess and Joe shot each other a quizzical look.

"We'll need to work on the details, obviously," Phineas continued, his excitement growing. "And the idea will sound rather eccentric to you perhaps. But that's just the sort of thing that will have the right effect on someone like Walter Huxley."

A broad grin appeared on his face as he looked from Joe to Bess.

Thirty-Two

"It's a harebrained scheme and it will never work," Joe grumbled while Bess sat at the table, writing the latest 'mysterious' note.

"I admit the plan is a bit odd," she replied without looking up from her work. "What was the word Phineas used? Eccentric?"

"That's just a fancy word for crazy. We should have gone with my plan. I still say simply beating a confession out of Huxley would've been the easiest way."

He was restlessly pacing the room. Bess wanted to tell him to sit down, because he was distracting her. But she knew Joe was more a man of action. Waiting and sitting around wasn't his strong side. So she just continued to write her note, slowly and methodically penning down the words in graceful, feminine letters.

"And my plan sure would have involved much less fluff and hassle than all of this." With a frustrated hand gesture, he waved at the things lying on the table: the sheets of luxurious note paper, the small creamy envelopes, the inkwell, the blotting paper and the bottle of perfume. He picked up the latter and looked at it like the exotic curiosity it was to him.

"Who even uses this stuff?" he asked. "I can understand why a lady would want to smell nice, but why waste it by sprinkling it on a piece of paper? Do you know how expensive this tiny bottle was? It's insane."

"Wait until you hear about the well-stocked armoury of creams, potions, powders and whatnots some ladies have at their disposal," she chuckled.

"Rich people are potty," he said, shaking his head in dismay. "Speaking of which, what's keeping Phineas? He's late. He said he'd be here at three."

"First of all," she smiled, "Phineas is neither rich, nor potty."

"Well, he's definitely odd."

"Secondly," she continued, ignoring Joe's nervous grumpiness, "He was supposed to be meeting Walter for luncheon today, so he's probably just been delayed."

Joe stopped his pacing and looked at her. "Do you honestly believe this plan of his is going to work, Bess? I mean, you writing these love notes from a dead woman? Surely, no man would be stupid enough to actually believe in them?"

She put down her pen carefully, to inspect her handiwork. A masterful piece of forgery, she thought approvingly.

"This is Walter Huxley we're talking about, Joe. He may be shrewd and clever in some respects, but when it comes to Rebecca and his sickening love for her, he's as gullible as they come."

"So you think he'll fall for it?"

She hesitated. Just like Joe, she had her doubts. But desperate times called for desperate measures, as the saying went. And she was desperate enough to try.

"See?" he said, pouncing on her brief pause. "You're not sure either. I knew it! Why don't you let me and the lads handle it? We'll have Huxley singing like a little canary in no time."

He hit his fist into the open palm of his other hand to illustrate what he meant.

"Joe, please," she replied gently. "I don't think that fighting murder and injustice with violence is the right answer."

He muttered under his breath and nodded impatiently. "Yes, I've heard all your arguments before. I just think–"

"I understand your concerns, Joe. You're worried because you care about me."

"Spot on! I don't want this to go wrong, Bess."

Reaching out to him, she placed a tender hand on his arm. "We have to try." Then she added jokingly, "And if we fail, we can always put your plan to the test."

"I'll hold you to that," he grinned.

They stood and smiled at each other, basking in the warmth of their friendship.

Suddenly, the door flew open and Tom barged in, panting, "Mr Parker is coming. We saw him rounding the corner just now."

"Excellent," Joe replied. "Let's see if he's got good news for us. My hands are beginning to itch."

Moments later, Phineas arrived. Seeing his smile brought Bess the relief she had been hoping for.

"I'm happy to report that our plan appears to be working so far," he said. "Walter seemed extremely nervous and jittery throughout the entire lunch. He really wasn't his usual boastful self. Constantly looking over his shoulder, forgetting what he was going to say mid-sentence, complaining about the air in the restaurant being too stuffy."

"Did he mention the notes?"

"No, but I'd say they're clearly having the desired effect."

"Unless," Joe objected, "Huxley was merely having an upset stomach."

Bess gave him a mildly annoyed look. "Let's, for argument's sake, assume it's our notes that were upsetting his tummy. What's our next step?"

"I think," Phineas said, "it's time for our grand finale. Have you written the note yet?"

She picked up the note she had just finished and waved it gently in the air to show him. "'Meet me at my final resting place at midnight tomorrow. Undyingly Yours, Rebecca,'" she repeated the words she had written. "It just needs a whiff of perfume once the ink has dried. Will you make the necessary arrangements with Chief Inspector White?"

Phineas nodded. "As soon as we are done here, I will personally go to his house to inform him of the time we have arranged. He said he would be ready with one of his men."

"That's another thing I don't like about this plan," Joe protested. "What's to stop this brass-buttoned copper from simply grabbing Bess?"

"He's given us his word of honour."

Joe snorted. "A peeler's word is absolutely worthless to me, Parker."

"I met the Chief Inspector once, Joe," Bess replied. "And he seemed like an honest man to me. Someone we can trust. And don't forget Rebecca had genuine affection for him. That's good enough for me."

"So you're telling me we should trust in your perception? Risk your life based on the sentiments of two people; one of whom –may I remind you?– is already dead!"

"The Chief Inspector was very receptive to our plan, Joe," Phineas intervened calmly. "He said my aunt had told him so many nice things about Bess, that he's very reluctant to believe Bess was the one who murdered Rebecca. And if we can get Walter to confess, the Chief Inspector will gladly clap the irons on the man."

"All right, all right," Joe grumbled, shoving his hands into his pockets. "But I want you both to know that I don't like it. At all."

"Fine," Bess replied with an amused grin. "As long as you promise to help us and play your part."

"Of course I will. The boys and I will be ready."

"Great," Phineas said. "That's settled then. Everybody knows what to do? We lure Walter to the cemetery with Rebecca's note and then we put on our little performance. The moment Walter confesses to the murder, the Chief Inspector and his man step forward and arrest the fellow."

"You make it sound so simple," she sighed.

"Too simple, if you ask me," Joe said.

"Don't worry, Bess," Phineas piped up cheerfully. "After tomorrow night, we will have cleared your name and you'll be a free woman again."

"Free," she repeated weakly. "I've almost forgotten what that feels like. I've been hiding away in here for so long, I can hardly bring myself round to believing I'll ever be free again."

"Tomorrow night, justice will be served," he assured her. "You'll see."

"Let's hope so," she murmured.

When Phineas gave her an encouraging smile, she tried to smile back. But from the corner of her eye, she could see Joe shaking his wary head. And she didn't know which of those two sentiments she agreed with most.

Thirty-Three

The hansom cab stopped on the corner of a quietly affluent street where all the residents and their servants had already retired for the night. A dense and chilly fog had come rolling in from the river earlier, draping the entire gaslit neighbourhood in an eerie atmosphere. Walter Huxley paid the driver, pulled the collar of his warm coat a little higher to obscure his face, and got out of the carriage.

"It's a horrible night, guv'nor," the driver complained. "There's something foul hiding in this fog. Better get inside quick if I were you."

Walter muttered his thanks and pretended to walk up to one of the front doors until the hansom had left. Then he turned and proceeded towards his real destination, which was only a short walking distance away. He had given the driver this address instead, because asking to be dropped off at the entrance of a cemetery at midnight would have raised suspicions.

The man had been right about the weather though, Walter grumbled inwardly. The fog made the streets treacherous and its icy wetness clung to everything, eventually creeping into the centre of your bones.

I must be mad for coming out here, he thought. *Just because a mysterious note asked me to.* Rebecca was dead. So how on earth could she be sending notes to him? The notion was absolutely preposterous!

'I'm writing to you from beyond the grave,' her first note had said. Thinking it was someone's poor idea of a joke, he had almost crumpled it up and thrown it into the fire. But even a year after her death, he was still obsessed with Rebecca Sutcliffe. And so, despite his head telling him it was simply impossible, he had kept the note – stowed away safely with the letters he had received from her in previous years.

Soon, more notes had followed, all claiming to be from Rebecca. He had studied them closely, comparing them with her other letters; the ones she had written to him during her life, when she thought she was replying to a fan letter from an anonymous admirer.

If these notes happened to be a forgery devised by some twisted individual, the differences should have been easy to spot. But the handwriting was a perfect match. The notes even smelled exactly like the letters had. They all had that heavenly scent, so strongly connected with Rebecca in his mind.

And yet, how could this be? The dead didn't come back, Walter told himself, even as he continued to hurry nervously towards the cemetery.

Or did they? Everybody knew the familiar stories about ghosts and spirits who were unable to rest when some sort of unfinished business kept them bound to the physical realm. Tall tales designed to thrill and entertain, obviously. But every story, no matter how incredible, often had an element of truth to it. And in Rebecca's case, Walter realised all too well why her eternal soul wouldn't want to rest.

Reaching the entrance of the graveyard, he paused and rested a hand on the closed iron gate. *Madness,* he repeated silently. *Sheer madness, this is.*

Perhaps the gate would be locked – in which case, he promised himself, he would simply return home and forget all about this absurd affair. *I'll even tear up those accursed notes and burn the shreds!*

But the old gate opened easily, be it with that typical metallic creaking noise every cemetery entrance seemed to make.

Gravel crunched and hissed underneath his patent leather shoes as he walked along the narrow paths that ran between the graves. There wasn't a soul around, living nor dead, he tried to reassure himself. But then why did his hair stand on end the way it did? In the daylight, these old cemeteries seemed such tranquil and peaceful places. Almost like a park where one could go for a quiet walk.

In the middle of the night however, surrounded by complete darkness and thick, fingerlike clouds of fog creeping close to the surface, he couldn't stop thinking about all those corpses of dead people lying under the very soil he was treading on.

He stopped in his tracks when he thought he heard a sound to his left. Pricking up his ears, he stood as still as a statue, convinced the beating of his anxious heart could be heard from miles away.

I should be safe at home, tucked up nice and warm in bed, he thought. *Not in this frighteningly morbid place on some fool's errand.*

He gave up listening to things that weren't there and sucked in a deep breath of ice-cold air, making his teeth chatter. *Steel yourself, Walter,* he said in his mind. *Go find Rebecca's grave and get it over with.* If the notes turned out to be a cruel prank, then at least his conscience could rest easy once more.

But if they were real...

That would mean he would get to see his beloved Rebecca again! However remote and improbable, he just couldn't let an opportunity like that slip him by. What would he say to her? Should he declare his undying love to her? Beg for her forgiveness?

He wasn't even sure if she would be able to communicate with him. In some stories, the spirits of the deceased were nothing but ghostly apparitions – mute phantoms who hovered and haunted in stillness. Maybe that would be better, he decided. To simply behold her face and her beauty again, without the need for any awkward words of apology. To approach her, silently, and gaze into her eyes. Sweet Lord, those green eyes of hers!

Oh Rebecca, why did you have to refuse my love? I didn't mean to hurt you that night. I would have given you everything your heart could have possibly desired. If only you had accepted.

A sudden fluttering of large dark wings in front of him made him cry out in terror. He covered his face with his hands and arms, certain that the

Angel of Death had come to take his blackened soul at last.

But when he lowered his hands again, he discovered that he had merely disturbed an owl feasting on its freshly caught prey. "Silly creature," he grumbled as he pressed on.

Finally, he came to the corner where Rebecca lay buried: a small clearing surrounded on two sides by trees and tall shrubs. He glanced around... and found no one.

But just as he was about to turn back to the main path, feeling half-relieved and half-disappointed, a veiled figure appeared from behind a private mausoleum and came striding slowly in the direction of Rebecca's grave.

He gasped. *Great heavens!*

Could it be true? Was it really her? Difficult to tell in the dark and with all this blasted fog. But that dress looked familiar. And the exotic fan she held up in front of her mouth and nose... Yes, he had seen those before! They were all part of Rebecca's costume in 'The Lady With The Painted Fan'.

Lord have mercy!

A hand came resting on his shoulder from behind, giving him such a fright he nearly soiled his breeches. He spun round and was surprised to see Phineas.

"I'm sorry, Walter," the young man whispered. "I didn't mean to startle you."

"Yet, startle me, you did," he replied, exhaling some of his tension. He turned back to where he had spotted the ghost and was relieved to see she was still there.

"Tragic, isn't it?" Phineas said, softly moving to Walter's side.

"Is that–?"

"Aunt Rebecca? Yes, it's her."

Enchanted by the ghostly figure, they watched her wandering aimlessly between the headstones.

"Did you get notes from her as well?" Walter asked.

"Notes?"

"Never mind." He paused and tried to comprehend this mystery. "But then, why are you here?"

"She's been visiting me in my dreams," Phineas replied. "Told me her spirit cannot rest as long as her murderer is still on the loose."

Walter swallowed. His throat felt awfully dry all of a sudden, as he began to wonder if he had made a mistake by coming here.

"Have you–" Cold sweat broke out on his forehead. "Have you been able to speak to her yet?"

Phineas shook his head. "I've tried, but she won't respond to me. Perhaps you should try?"

"Me?! Why?"

"Because you loved her and she loved you back. She wanted to be your bride. Isn't that what you said at the trial?"

"Yes, but–"

"Then call out to her now," Phineas urged.

"I– I can't. I'm afraid my legs and my voice will fail me."

"Walter, please," Phineas pleaded. "Spirits often know more than we mortals do. She might know where her murderer is hiding. Let us go to her together, so we can ask her to lead us to her killer."

"No!" His cheeks quivered when he fervently shook his head.

"Walter, calm yourself. She may be a ghost, but we have nothing to fear from her. It's her murderer she wants."

"I don't want to speak to her," he trembled.

"But why not? I don't understand." Phineas looked at him, with those same friendly green eyes as his aunt's.

He wanted to tell the boy. Or at least hint at his real reasons. So the poor lad might grasp why it was simply out of the question to approach Rebecca's ghost.

But he couldn't. The truth was too painful, too ugly –and too dangerous– to ever be revealed.

"Walter?" Phineas was still staring at him, with a soft and imploring look.

He licked his cold, dry lips.

"I..."

Should he? What if–

Suddenly, he heard a high-pitched startled cry and they both turned their heads – just in time to see the ghost stumbling over a gravestone.

"That didn't sound like Rebecca," Walter said. He looked at Phineas, who seemed anxious and at a loss for words. "What is the meaning of this?"

He took a step in the direction of the so-called ghost who was trying to get back on her feet, whimpering in a voice he still recognised.

Phineas grabbed his arm to stop him. "Walter, no."

"So now you *don't* want me to speak to your ghost, eh?" he growled.

With an angry jerk, he pulled his arm away from Phineas' grip and stomped over to the dishevelled phantom figure.

Thirty-Four

Bess cursed herself for tripping over that stupid gravestone. Now she had spoiled their plan. Before she had time to think, a furious-looking Walter was already upon her, brutally grabbing hold of her arm and tearing off the veil that had hidden her face.

"You," he growled viciously. "I knew it was your voice! Why, you dirty street louse? Why did you do this?"

As he stood shaking her, the cemetery that had previously seemed so quiet and deserted came to life. From one side, a young man and three boys leapt out of the bushes.

"Let go of her, you coward," Joe shouted while they rushed towards Bess and Walter.

From the other side, a man emanating a natural air of imposing authority strode urgently towards them. A police constable with a menacing scowl followed right behind him, and Phineas was quick to join the two.

"Mr Huxley, I am Chief Inspector White," the man called out to Walter. "We would like to have a word with you."

Beleaguered from all sides, Walter turned to Bess and hissed, "So that's what's going on, is it? A trap!" There was hatred in his voice. But his eyes were cold. Cold and deadly.

His hand lashed out and struck her in the face. "I should have strangled *you* instead," he said before shoving her to the ground and running away.

"Jones, after him," Chief Inspector White barked at his constable, who immediately gave chase.

Bess was clambering back to her feet when they all reached her, everyone talking over each other and asking her if she was hurt.

"I'm fine," she said. "Just a bit bruised and shaken, that's all. Phineas, I'm so sorry. I've ruined your plan."

In the distance, they could hear the shrill police whistle of Constable Jones.

"All's not lost, Miss Morgan," the inspector spoke confidently. "We might yet get Mr Huxley to confess."

"You'll have to catch him first," Joe scoffed. He gave his boys a sharp nod of the head. "Run, lads.

Follow the sound of that whistle. Go get the blighter!"

Like howling mad hounds, Georgie, Tom and Bill dashed in the direction Walter and the constable had taken.

"Parker, are you coming too?" Joe asked, pausing impatiently.

"Yes, hurry," the inspector urged the two young men. "I'll bring up Miss Morgan as quickly as we can."

Phineas and Joe took off together, while Chief Inspector White offered Bess a hand. "Can you walk, Miss?"

"I'll trot and gallop," she answered doggedly, "if that's what it takes to catch Walter."

"That's the spirit," the inspector grinned. "Reminds me of a certain lady I once knew."

The two of them ran to the cemetery gate and stopped in the middle of the street, looking left and right, trying to figure out which way the hunt for Walter was heading.

Just then, someone appeared at the far corner and whistled on his fingers to get their attention. "Follow me," Georgie shouted. "He tried to cross the bridge, but we've got him trapped."

Darting after the little boy, Bess and the inspector soon came to a stone bridge spanning the river. The side nearest to them was being guarded by Phineas and Joe with his two older boys, while a handful of policemen blocked off the other side. Bess saw Walter a bit further on the bridge, standing on the thick stone railing. Looking agitated, he kept glancing to and fro between the two groups that had him cornered.

"Don't come any nearer or I'll jump," he shouted.

When Constable Jones spotted his superior, he hurried over to report. "My whistle attracted the assistance of a few colleagues as you can see, Chief Inspector. We're awaiting your further instructions, sir."

The inspector stepped a bit closer to Walter and called out, "Don't do anything foolish, Mr Huxley. We just want to have a little chat with you."

"Why me? I'm innocent. There's your murderer," Walter yelled back, pointing at Bess. "She was found guilty by the court. Arrest her, not me."

White raised his hand, gesturing to his men to hold off. "Who said anything about arresting you, Mr Huxley? Why would we need to do that?"

"Well played, Chief Inspector. But you won't trick me that easily."

Bess took a few steps closer as well now. "Why did you do it, Walter?" she cried bitterly. "Why did you kill Rebecca?"

"No no no no. I didn't do it," Walter laughed. "Not me, no. *You* did, remember? The jury and the judge, they all said so."

"I would never have hurt Rebecca! I loved her." Warm, salty tears were streaming down her face as their angry exchange grew more heated.

"So did I," Walter replied. "I loved her just as much as you did. Even more!"

"No, you didn't. What you felt for Rebecca wasn't love. You wanted to own her. You were jealous. Jealous of all the others who received more attention and more affection from her than you could ever hope for."

"Lies," he shrieked furiously.

"Jealous," she shot back savagely. "Jealous of her lovers. Jealous of her admirers. And jealous of me. Weren't you?"

"Yes, I was! There, I've said it. I was jealous. I loved Rebecca long before she became famous and everyone started vying for her favour. I worshipped that woman like the queen and the goddess she was. And like a grovelling worm, I worshipped the ground she walked on."

Walter's face was red with pure rage, while Bess stood and listened as he continued to hurl his words at her.

"But she never loved me back," he moaned pathetically. "Every time I hinted at love or marriage, she giggled and laughed and told me I was silly. I could have given her a comfortable life, but she said she wanted her freedom. She would sooner entertain those wealthy swine than marry the man who truly cared for her."

"What happened that night outside The Blue Boar, Walter?" The question had escaped her mouth before she realised it. But Walter's frenzied mind was too far gone to notice the danger it posed to himself.

"The success of her play had made her absolutely ecstatic with joy. I thought she looked even more attractive than ever before. It was like she had this golden halo of supernatural beauty about her. And I simply had to have her for my own. So when we were finally alone at the end of the night, I laid my heart before her feet and asked her to marry me."

"And she refused you? Again."

"Yes, she did," he spat angrily. "Again! Only this time, she laughed at me. Not a sweet and innocent giggle like she used to do. But a hard and hurtful cackle, full of contempt. Afterwards, I realised she had been drinking too much and that she probably didn't mean it that way. But in that moment, by the side of that dark and lonely alley..."

"What, Walter? What happened?"

His eyes were hazy and it seemed as if his mind was elsewhere, hovering between worlds.

"I went mad. Quite simply mad. I just wasn't myself anymore. It was like a demon had entered my body. My hands found her throat and squeezed." As if he were reliving the scene, his hands went up to some invisible throat... and closed around it.

"I squeezed and I squeezed so hard. She tried to struggle for a bit, but she was too surprised, I think. I can still see the look of horror in her eyes. Those beautiful, mesmerising green eyes. Then, she stopped struggling, the light vanished from her eyes, and her body went limp."

"So you left her there?" Bess felt sick to the stomach, listening to this deranged murderer.

He nodded slowly, all passion and energy having deserted him. "Once I realised what I'd done, I panicked. I dragged her body into the alley, hoping no one had seen us. As she lay there in the dirt, I spotted her necklace... and I took it. I snatched it off her neck, because I wanted to have a token to remember her by, forever."

Sad and relieved to have finally learned the horrible truth, Bess broke down in tears and buried her face in her hands.

Silently, Chief Inspector White stepped forward and placed a gentle hand on her shoulder.

"Walter Huxley, I'm arresting you for the murder of Miss Rebecca Sutcliffe, to which you have just confessed in the presence of all these witnesses. Step down from that railing, please, so we may escort you to the nearest police station."

The inspector's voice caused Walter to snap out of his delirious memories. "Never, you hear," he laughed hysterically. "I'll never let you take me. No one has the right to make Walter Huxley go through the humiliation of a public trial. And hanging is an awful way to go. Unspeakably awful! Men like me, we die by our own hand."

He glanced at the abyss below him and stepped over the edge of the stone railing, into the bleak void of the night.

They heard his shrieking death cry all the way down, until his body hit the rushing waters of the Thames.

Everybody ran to the spot where he had jumped and peered over the side. But there was no more trace of him.

"They don't usually survive a drop like that, sir," Constable Jones said. "And even when they do, the river soon finishes the job. Some unlucky fisherman or a mudlark scouring the riverbanks will probably find his body in a few days."

The Chief Inspector nodded. "Alert our colleagues of the River Police." Then he turned to Bess and her friends, and said, "You will all need to come to the station with us."

Little Georgie bravely stepped in between her and the inspector, declaring, "You're not taking Bess from us, Mr Policeman!"

The Chief Inspector smiled. "We need your statements about what you have heard and witnessed here tonight."

"And after that?" Joe demanded.

"Miss Morgan will need to go through the courts to get her name cleared."

"No," Phineas protested. "What if they decide to hang her anyway?"

"That won't happen," the chief inspector said. "It will only be a matter of formalities. I promise I shall personally see to it."

Joe opened his mouth to speak, but the inspector went on, "In the meantime, I don't see any need to keep Miss Morgan in a cell. As soon as we have your witness accounts written down, you and she are free to go."

Free, the word echoed in her mind.

Was it true? Had her nightmare finally ended?

Thirty-Five

The sun had already begun to colour the sky with its morning hues of pink and orange by the time Bess and her friends left the police station. They were tired from their ordeal, but their hearts felt light with a sense of peace and closure. Slowly and with nowhere in particular to go, they walked in silence for a short spell, cherishing each other's closeness.

"I'm hungry," Georgie said after a while.

"I think we all are, little man," Phineas replied kindly. "Why don't we go for a decent breakfast together? My treat."

A smile appeared on Georgie's face, brighter than the brightest sunrise. "I hope you've got a lot of money on you, sir. Because Bill, Tom and me, we could just about eat a horse right now."

The grown-ups laughed and Joe fished a few coins from his pockets. "Here, you lads go and buy something to eat from that man at the stall on the corner for now. That way, the rest of us can have a conversation without your bellies rumbling."

Bill deftly caught the coins Joe tossed at him and then the three boys ran off while Bess, Phineas and Joe continued at a more relaxed pace.

"How can they have so much energy left after a night like that?" Phineas smiled. He was walking to the right of Bess, with Joe on her left.

"That's hardened street boys for you, Parker," Joe replied. "How does it feel to be free again, Bess?"

"I'm not sure it's sunk in yet," she said with a feeble grin. "Did last night really happen or was it just a dream? It's still so hard to believe."

"It happened," Phineas said. "And I'm glad it did."

"Same," Joe agreed. "Huxley was even more insane than I imagined. He sounded like a madman who had lost his mind."

"Perhaps he had," Bess mused. "He was always weak to begin with. Maybe the guilt of what he had done and the fear of being found out ended up breaking him."

"It's a shame he took his own life," Phineas said. "He should have faced justice."

"Oh, I don't know," Joe said. "Him jumping in the river to kill himself– It's a kind of justice that appeals more to me than if we had handed him over to the police. More natural this way."

"That's just because you don't like the police, Joe," Bess chuckled.

"True enough! I spent so much time hanging around policemen last night, I don't want to see another uniform for weeks. So I might just need to stay off the streets for a while."

"Goodness me," she exclaimed jokingly. "You really must have had your fill then, for you to want to take a break from your usual thieving and picking pockets."

"I suppose I'm getting old," he laughed. "Before you know it, I'll be wanting to settle down and become an honest man. It's shocking."

"That would be quite the shock indeed," she chortled. "In earnest though, wouldn't you want to do something different with your life? Something... more rewarding – and less dangerous?"

He shrugged. "The trouble is, what else is there? I like money and I'd love to be rich, but I'm nowhere near as talented or educated as you two."

"You mustn't say that, Joe," Phineas objected. "Everyone has talents and skills."

"Maybe. I just don't see what mine are, that's all."

"Oh, come now, Joe," Bess said. "You're clever, you're witty and you're charming. And whether you want to admit it or not, you have a big heart. You love to help people."

"Thank you kindly, my lady," Joe quipped with a short bow of the head. "I'll keep your advice in mind. But what about you, my dear Bess? What will you do now that you don't have to hide from the Law anymore?"

"I don't know yet," she sighed. "Rebecca was everything to me. I never had imagined a life without her."

Joe nodded, pensively staring ahead of him. "These things take time. Have you given any thought to getting married and raising a family?"

Smiling awkwardly, she stammered, "Joe, I–"

"Don't worry, I wasn't talking about me, you know." He paused and purposefully cleared his throat. After another brief silence, he said, "For Pete's sake, Parker. Don't make her wait all day for it. Pipe up, man!"

"Wh–what?" Phineas stuttered. "I don't– I don't understand."

Joe rolled his eyes and halted. "All right, I'll spell it out for you then. You and I both like Bess. But it's obvious she and I can never be more than friends."

"Best friends," she insisted.

He gave her an appreciative smile and turned back to Phineas. "You and her though, well, in case you hadn't noticed yet, you're made for each other."

Bess and Phineas both blushed and exchanged a quick, shy glance.

"See?" Joe said, seizing the moment. "That's the sort of thing I'm talking about. You're both so clearly in love that, quite frankly, I'm amazed you haven't proposed to the girl yet, Parker."

Bess giggled nervously.

"As a matter of fact," Phineas said, "I asked her if we could court, just before this whole… unpleasant business started."

"Courtship is a start, I guess," Joe frowned, before giving him an encouraging look.

"Bess," Phineas started, positioning himself in front of her and taking her hands in his.

Joe discreetly turned his back to them and moved a few steps away, pretending to admire some interesting architectural features on a nearby building.

"Phineas?" she replied, expectantly, as her heart began to beat faster.

"You've known how I feel about you for more than a year now. And those feelings haven't changed. Not on my part anyway."

"My feelings for you are still the same as well, Phineas. To tell you the truth, they have only grown stronger lately."

"My dearest Bess, it would give me great pleasure, and it would be a tremendous honour, if you would agree to be joined with me in holy matrimony and become my wife."

Standing a few paces away, Joe coughed and murmured, "Oi, Mr Playwright. Plain English, please."

Phineas blushed and Bess giggled. Then he cleared his throat and gazed into her eyes.

"Bess, will you marry me?"

"Yes, Phineas–my love, my angel! I will marry you."

A glorious smile of blissful joy rose all the way up from his mouth to his sparkling green eyes. Oblivious to the world around her, she felt herself being drawn into his gaze and she wanted to taste the sweetness of his tender lips.

But then the three boys returned, boisterously noisy while licking pastry crumbs off their fingers. When Georgie saw a blushing Bess and

Phineas disengage from their embrace, he asked, "What's going on?"

"Good news, lads," Joe said cheerfully. "Mr Parker has just proposed to Miss Morgan."

"Bess is going to marry Mr Parker?!"

"Yes, she is," Joe replied. "Isn't that great?"

"I suppose," the little boy said with a slight pout.

"What's the matter, Georgie?" Bess asked fondly.

"Nothing," he lied and shrugged.

Bess raised one eyebrow and smiled, "Nothing?"

"I'm glad Mr Parker wants to marry you, of course. And I'm very happy that the police have stopped searching for you. But, well—"

"You're sad to see me leave you and Bill and Tom and Joe, is that it?"

He nodded, ashamed of his feelings. "I was so enjoying learning to read and write, Bess. And I loved your cooking lessons."

"Yeah," Tom said. "I'll miss the cooking too."

"But that doesn't need to stop, my darlings," she assured them. "I'm sure we can work something out. Just because Mr Parker and I are getting married doesn't mean I can't teach you about letters and numbers, or cooking and good manners. Isn't that right, Phineas?"

"Absolutely. And to add a bit of culture to your education, we'll give you free tickets to all the plays Bess and I will be producing."

"Hmm," Joe said, rubbing his chin. "Lots of rich toffs in the audience, I reckon?"

"Oh Joe, please," she pleaded. "You mustn't go round picking people's pockets at our performances. That would be frightfully awkward for Phineas and me."

"Are you telling me I'm not allowed to profit from rubbing elbows with the rich and famous? How inconsiderate of you, Bess," he said, pretending to feel hurt.

"Joe, promise me you won't steal from anyone or pick any pockets when you come to our plays."

"All right then," he agreed. Grinning impishly, he turned to Phineas. "All of a sudden I'm feeling very grateful that I'm not the one who's marrying her, Parker. You've got a strong-minded woman on your hands here, my good friend."

"Joe Thompson!" she bristled at him in jest.

"Aunt Rebecca has taught her well," Phineas laughed.

"Excuse me," little Georgie said. "Can we go and have that breakfast we were promised now, please?" He eyed Bess and Phineas suspiciously. "Or will you be kissing first?"

"I must admit the thought of breakfast sounds very appealing to me at the moment," Bess giggled.

Slipping her hands around Phineas' arm, she whispered in his ear, "I hope the kissing can wait a little longer?"

Phineas smiled and stared at her with a mysterious twinkle in his emerald eyes.

Perhaps not too long then, she thought.

Epilogue

Years later...

Strolling leisurely, Bess did a slow round along the walls of the empty lobby of The Grand Theatre. She knew the curtain would soon be falling over the play that was currently being performed on the stage. If she strained her ears, she thought she could hear the muffled sounds of the actors' voices delivering their lines of the closing scene. She wasn't able to make out the actual words, but she knew those by heart anyway, having been present at so many rehearsals.

Closing her eyes, she tried to picture Abbie, awfully young but formidable in her very first leading role. In her mind's eye, she could see the elegant actress standing centre-stage in her exquisite costume dress, personally designed and made by Bess – right down to the very last seam.

When the play was over, the crowd would come streaming into the lobby from the sold-out auditorium, the galleries and the expensive box seats. But for now, the grand hall with its domed ceiling was blissfully quiet and peaceful. She loved these moments. They gave her a bit of time to be alone with her thoughts – and her memories.

Passing by a large brass commemorative plaque, her fingers drifted dreamily across the engraved letters that stated this theatre was restored and renovated in loving tribute to the late Miss Rebecca Sutcliffe.

She stopped and caressed the name of the woman who had meant so much to her.

Then her hand went to her slightly bulging belly, when she thought she felt the baby kicking its leg in there. "I know, little darling," she smiled. "It's time we went to see your Papa and your big sister, isn't it?"

She wound her way backstage, where she quickly spotted her husband and their young daughter Rosie. The two were holding hands as they breathlessly watched the play's final scene from the obscurity of the wings.

When the play came to an end and the curtain closed, the audience erupted in a rousing applause that never failed to move Bess. *Just like old times,* a voice from the past sounded in her mind.

"Papa," Rosie exclaimed, jumping up and down in her wild excitement. "They love it!" Looking round to tell any other member of the crew nearby, she caught sight of her mother.

"Mama! Can you hear that? People love Papa's new play!"

Bess strode over to them, kissed a beaming Phineas and bent down towards her little girl as far as her belly allowed. "I know. Isn't it wonderful, darling?"

She gave her daughter an affectionate kiss. "They love it, because Papa is such a gifted writer and a brilliant producer."

"Yes, he is," Rosie nodded proudly, before feeling obliged to quickly add, "But of course, it's also because of the beautiful costumes you designed, Mama."

"Miss Lee did brilliantly," Phineas smiled at his wife. "Just like you said she would, dearest."

"I told you I had every faith in her," Bess replied. "Abbie may be young, but she's insanely talented."

After the cast had taken their bows and performed their encores, they came rushing from the stage, grinning from ear to ear and buzzing with an electrifying frenzy that seemed to infect everyone backstage. Bess and Phineas congratulated each of them individually, before the actors disappeared in the dressing rooms to change into their own clothes.

"There's Uncle Joe," Rosie shouted cheerfully when she spotted their old family friend popping round for a backstage visit. "Did you see Papa's play, Uncle Joe?"

"I sure did, my cheeky little angel. Your Papa and Mama give me free tickets for every single one of their opening nights, remember?"

He picked her up by the waist and lifted her up into the air with his strong arms, making her squeal and giggle with delight.

"Are Bill and Tom here as well?" Rosie asked after he had put her down again.

"Yes, I left them in the lobby and the bar area, to mingle with the important people."

Phineas chuckled. "Always ready to do business, eh, you sly fox?"

"Why, evidently, old man," Joe grinned.

Rosie tugged at her mother's sleeve. "If Papa and Uncle are going to be talking about money and business again, may I go and help Mrs Roberts tidy up the costumes in the dressing room, please?"

"Yes, you may, darling," Bess said.

The three of them watched the girl dash off to the dressing rooms in a rush of lovely thick curls and rich, rustling fabrics.

"If ever a girl was worthy of the name Rose," Joe smiled. "And where's little Philip?"

"At home, with the nanny," Phineas replied. "He's too young still to come to these affairs."

"So is Rosie, to be fair," Bess chortled. "But no one could possibly have kept her from attending the opening night of her Papa's new play."

"As feisty as her mama, is she?" Joe teased, to the laughter of Phineas.

"Old charmer," Bess joked back. "Just you wait until the day you're blessed with children of your own. Heaven forbid they should take after their father."

"I'm as sweet as a little lamb," Joe said, pretending to be hurt.

"Hardly," Bess snorted. "I distinctly remember you being a roguish street thug in your pickpocketing days."

"Good times," he laughed. "Being in finance is a bit like picking people's pockets, you know. Only it's legal and much more lucrative."

"You're certainly very good at it, Joe," Phineas said.

"At what? Picking people's pockets?" he grinned rakishly. "I haven't done that in years, my friend."

"No," Bess giggled. "Phineas means finance, you silly sausage. And I think you're even better at that than you ever were at picking pockets."

Joe shrugged. "All I really do is talk. I talk to people who have ideas, and I talk to people who have money. And then, I simply connect the right dots, make a few connections... and receive my commission."

He had made it sound as if it was child's play. But Bess saw the cheeky twinkle in his eye. He lived for the hunt.

"I, for one, think you do it exceedingly well, all this talking," she said. "After all, it's thanks to you that we managed to find the investors to buy The Grand and renovate it."

"Hear hear", Phineas agreed. "We owe you an eternal debt of gratitude, Joe."

"You don't owe me anything, my dear friends. Just keep those free tickets coming for me and the lads. Your performances tend to draw the wealthiest crowds and the most eccentric people."

"Who's eccentric?" a beautiful young lady asked as she appeared by Bess' side. "Mrs Parker, won't you please do me the honour of introducing this kind gentleman to me?"

"But of course," Bess smiled broadly. "Mr Joe Thompson, please meet Miss Abigail Lee, our newest leading lady and soon-to-be star."

"How do you do?" Abbie cooed.

"How do you do?" Joe returned her greeting with a respectful nod of the head and an appreciative glimmer in his eyes.

"Mr Thompson, you say?" Abbie asked. "Why does that name sound familiar to me?"

"Perhaps," Bess replied, "because you've seen it on that great big plaque in our lobby."

When Abbie frowned and tilted her head slightly, Phineas explained, "It was Mr Thompson who most graciously took it upon himself to find sponsors and benefactors to renovate the theatre. And that's why his name is mentioned on the commemorative plaque."

Abbie's eyes opened wide. "Oh, my! Are you *that* Mr Thompson?"

"The very same," Joe replied, bowing like a gentleman while bringing her hand to his lips for a civilised kiss.

"Are you a banker then, Mr Thompson?"

"Better than that, my dear. I get to play with other people's money."

"That sounds marvellously exciting, sir. You simply must tell me all about it."

"I'd be happy to, Miss. Might I be so bold as to invite you to dinner? You must be starving after that exceptional performance of yours."

"I must admit the stage takes quite a bit out of me," she replied melodramatically. "But you liked it, did you, Mr Thompson?" She batted her eyelashes and fixed her great big eyes on him.

He doesn't stand a chance against her charms, Bess thought with glee, as she tried to keep a straight face.

"Stellar performance, Miss Lee," Joe said. "Simply and delightfully stellar."

"Why, thank you, Mr Thompson. Too kind of you, sir. Are you a great lover of the theatre?"

"I'm a lover of many of the finer things in life, Miss Lee. Theatre, art... beauty." At the latter, he stared intensely at her.

"Oh, Mr Thompson. You sound like such a refined and distinguished gentleman. I feel like I could listen to you for hours."

"Then I suggest we dine at the Chateau d'Or, where we can discuss art, beauty and life for as long as we like."

"Isn't that where you got Georgie a position as the chef's senior apprentice?" Bess asked.

"It is," Joe said proudly.

"How is he getting along there? Is he enjoying himself?"

"Tremendously. I might just buy the restaurant for him once he's a bit older." He turned to Abbie and smiled, "It's the least a man can do for a talented lad like him."

"Is he your son, Mr Thompson?" she enquired not so innocently.

"No, Georgie is what you might call my ward. I've been looking after him since he was a little boy, haven't I, Mrs Parker?"

Bess nodded.

"How generous of you, Mr Thompson," Abbie cooed. "Haven't you got any children of your own then? A man like you must be married, surely."

"Alas, no! You might say I'm still looking for love, Miss Lee."

She opened her fan, waved some cool air in her face and then made a vague attempt to hide her coquettish smile behind the fan.

"You poor thing, Mr Thompson."

"I seek to bear my hardship with grace, Miss Lee," he replied as he proffered his arm to her. Abbie promptly wrapped her hands around it, like a well-mannered lady.

"Mr and Mrs Walker," Joe said, "if you'll excuse us, please. I need to inform my two associates of an important engagement that has just cropped up this evening."

After the smiling couple-to-be had taken their leave of them, Bess and Phineas waited until the pair had disappeared from view, before bursting out in laughter.

"I don't know who I should be feeling more sorry for," Phineas chuckled. "Poor Joe or sweet Abbie?"

"Feel sorry for them?" Bess said, giggling with mirth. "Why darling, they're absolutely made for each other!"

"Do you think so?"

"But of course! They'll each try to tame and control the other. There will be fireworks between them every single day and they'll drive each other up the wall."

Phineas frowned, "Now I'm beginning to feel sorry for both of them."

"Haven't you seen the sparkle in their eyes? I think Joe Thompson has finally found his match. Take it from me: this is the birth of true love we've just witnessed."

"I think you might be right," Phineas laughed. "Perhaps we should write a play about them: 'The Mermaid and The Merchant: A Tale of Passion About The Quest for Veritable Love.'"

"Shall I start designing the costumes then, dear?" Bess quipped.

Phineas took her in his arms and said, "I'm sure it can wait until tomorrow morning. First, I want to take my darling wife and my lovely daughter home. And then, when we've put the children to bed, you and I can have a quiet little celebration of our own. Tonight has been brilliant."

She nodded. Captivated by the infamously mesmerising gaze of his emerald eyes, she swooned and let out the world's most blissful sigh.

The End

Continue reading...

If you enjoyed this book, you will love Hope Dawson's other romance stories as well.

Visit www.hopedawson.com for updates and to *claim your free digital book*.

Other titles by Hope:

The Forgotten Daughter
The Carter's Orphan
The Millworker's Girl
The Ratcatcher's Daughter
The Foundling With The Flowers
The Pit Brow Sisters
The Dockside Orphans
The Christmas Foundling
The Girl Below Stairs
The Market Girl's Secret
The Blind Sibling

Printed in Great Britain
by Amazon